Happy Christmas 1975
from
M. Taylor

Lydia M. Clarke
Eddiston Farm
Iain·

LENT TERM

Confronted by the loneliness which descends after her five children have all gone to school, Alison Osmond, the middle-aged wife of a North country clergyman, is forced to realise the lack of communication and desolation in her married life. While she respects her husband Ken's withdrawn temperament, she throws upon him the responsibility for upholding ideals for them both and so preventing disaster.

On a trip to the North country town of Pendale to attend a diocesan council meeting, Alison accepts a lift with the Dean, George Tindall. In a moment of sexual abandon she starts a flirtation with him to prove that in spite of his apparent indifference she can attract him; and beneath the austere front he presents she discovers a passionate and turbulent being she never knew existed. Their affair develops and they sleep one night together as man and wife. Unaware of her true feelings towards him, Alison discards him brutally and denies the effect of the small matter of adultery as a moment of generous lust she could afford to give in to.

However her action has profound repercussions in the lives of them both.

Elizabeth Sutherland

Lent Term

Constable London

First published in Great Britain 1973
by Constable and Company Ltd
10 Orange Street London WC2H 7EG
Copyright © 1973 by Elizabeth Sutherland

ISBN 0 09 459170 9

Reprinted 1974

To my daughter-in-law, Jane,
who has always been so encouraging

Printed and bound in Great Britain by
REDWOOD BURN LIMITED
Trowbridge & Esher

I

The attic bedroom smelled of old socks, bay-rum hair oil and rotten apples. Alison regarded the debris of invention, improvisation and rejection with a sense of desolation. For thirteen years, her youngest son's life had been contained in this chilly upper room. Without him, it was as squalid as a dustbin.

There were four other similar rooms situated on the top floor of the aged dilapidated vicarage, but none of them filled her with such a sense of loss as this. For twenty years, there had been boys in varying numbers who had pounded the floors, creaked the rafters and generally demanded her attention. Now, since this morning there were none. It was so still that she could hear the grandfather clock ticking in the hall two flights down.

She picked up an empty polythene sack and began to stuff it with comics, toffee papers, bits of balsa wood, the bowels of old radios and the distorted remains of well-chewed gum. There were the kitchen scissors missing since Christmas, and that disgusting brown mush in the old washing-up bowl behind the wardrobe must be the end product of the cider-making session that had started with a glut of apples in the autumn.

She stripped the bed and sat down on the hard hair mattress and yawned, for it had been an exhausting week full of last minute rushes to the barber and the dentist. The

5

previous night, she had taken her student sons to catch the night train to their respective university towns, and that morning she had taken the three younger boys to catch the school train. This was the day she had secretly dreaded for years and now that it had come it was as bad, if not worse than she had imagined. Without any of her sons, she did not know how she was going to exist till the Easter holidays.

Ken had told her at lunch to leave the clearing up to another time, but she knew she could not relax until the floors were swept, drawers tidied and beds stripped. There was something unbearably sad about the dusty clutter of her sons' possessions. She knew the load of depression would not lift from her heart until she had transformed the rooms from tombs to cosy nests ready for the returning fledglings.

As she put the discarded holiday clothing into a pile for washing, she thought about her youngest son. He would still be in the train, having, no doubt, eaten half a term's supply of home-made sweets and cakes. Protected by the presence of two of his brothers he would be irresponsibly excited and cheeky. All the same, she knew that in the pit of his tight little stomach there crawled the worm of dread and homesickness. His childhood was over, ended as abruptly as her motherhood. The boy who would come back to her in three months' time would not need her in the same total way that he had needed her up to this day. She wondered if she had given him as much happiness as he had given her. Looking back, she was appalled at the thought of how little she had given him of herself and her time. She could only hope that it had been enough.

How little she had given any of her sons, if it came to that, and yet, being what she was, she could have given no more. There had been so many of them with their hopes and dreads and demands, and only one mother to cope with them. Her heart yearned for their vulnerability, as well as for her own inadequacy. Feeling the sting of tears, she hurried into the next room.

The empty shell of a vast amplifier occupied the whole of one wall. It was stacked with records, pop magazines, copies of *Exchange and Mart* well-thumbed at the musical instrument offers. An old guitar-string threaded with dust lay beneath the bed. Pictures of way-out pop groups adorned the walls which had been painted scarlet and black, giving the room the appearance of a hot cellar in mid-winter. She switched on the light to find that the bulb had been painted yellow, giving the room a weird glare. She exchanged the bulb for the one in the passage and once again began the dreary task of clearing-up. The room belonged to her second eldest and she found he had left a note-book full of diagrams and calculations which she put on one side to post together with the toothbrush and shaving kit he had left in the bathroom. During the course of the next few days, there would be five parcels in the post. Each of the children always forgot something important. Ken maintained that, subconsciously, they were leaving part of themselves, the small aching part that did not want to leave home. Personally, she put their forgetfulness down to the fact that she always included something to eat in the return parcel.

And yet she would not have wished them back, at least not all of them. She needed the three months of peace to pick up the pieces of her own personality. It was hard work mentally and physically bringing up five children so close in years and so diverse and demanding in personality. She would have liked one of them, preferably the youngest, to brighten the tired old house and to lighten her loneliness. Often in the past, she had held her hands to her ears to shut out the racket of laughter or bickering; now she realised that even the minor riots that sometimes disrupted the house for hours were preferable to this silence.

'Anyone at home?'

A door banged and she heard Clem's tread on the attic stairs.

'My God, don't they teach them tidiness in those expensive educational establishments, or are they so repressed there that when they come home they revert to the primitive!'

Clem held vaguely socialistic ideas where children were concerned but was unashamedly snobbish about the breeding and upbringing of dogs.

'They take after their parents,' said Alison smiling.

'Don't tell me boys still use this?' Clem held up a bottle of bay-rum hair lotion stickily coated with dust. 'I thought it had gone out with short hair and the Beatles.'

The griffon in the blue knitted jacket sneezed.

'Precious Honey!' She picked up the little dog. 'Did all that nasty dust give him an allergy then?'

Alison laughed. 'You are an ass over that dog. Let's go downstairs and have some tea. I'm ready for it. Mrs Bews can finish here in the morning.'

She opened the door of her eldest son's room and pushed in the vacuum cleaner.

'And let her find this?'

Clem held up a paper carrier-bag printed with the Union Jack and stuffed full of old beer cans.

'You must be mad. The whole village will know by the following morning that the vicar's eldest son is a dypso-maniac.' She put the bag in the rubbish sack and took off her coat. 'Come on, let's get it done while you're in the mood.'

She began to stack girlie magazines and lurid paper-backs into the bookcase.

'Do you really approve of all this?' she asked, indicating the beer and the books. 'What is more to the point, does Ken approve?'

'I don't suppose he knows,' she replied, plugging in the switch for the vacuum.

She supposed she ought to disapprove of the beer, the busty women and the cigarette stubs in the Coca-Cola dregs, but she could not bring herself to worry. As long as the boys were well, hurt neither themselves nor anyone else, passed the necessary exams, she no longer minded much what they did. As a mother of small boys, she had cared too much; afraid of their untamed manners in congregational drawing-rooms, ashamed of their restlessness in church, shocked at their perpetual bickering behaviour among themselves. She had so exhausted herself fretting over details that by the time they reached boarding-school age, she was thankful to hand them over to paid disciplinarians, and let the niceties of behaviour go by the board in the holidays. By the time the youngest child reached adolescence, nothing shocked her and what had once seemed so important to her – a veneer of manners and scrupulous attention to mental and physical cleanness – had become practically meaningless. She wondered if Clem sensed that the slovenliness of her boys, as judged by their rooms, stemmed initially from her. Dear shockable Clem who screamed if her dog piddled on the carpet.

She switched off the vacuum and began to strip the bed. Clem bent down to pick up a particularly explicit pin-up picture.

'Good God,' she said, 'look at those bosoms!'

The two women stared at the mounds of naked flesh.

9

'They do it with silicone, or is it foam rubber?' Clem said thoughtfully. 'How different it all is nowadays. My brother would probably have been sent to the colonies on a remittance if he had left this lying about for my mother to see. How lucky they are – the young I mean. Everything's permitted; everything's geared to their amusement. What wouldn't I give to be young again.'

'Hideous thought,' Alison said, remembering her strict childhood fenced round with rules and behaviour patterns; the convent school where there was freedom only to study and play team games; the emotional dramas and guilt complexes.

'Ah, but what I really mean is to be young in body – and, incidentally, my bust was just as good as that photograph – and old, or at any rate comfortably middle-aged in experience,' Clem explained as she groped for a pea-nut shell wedged in the wainscoting. 'What a combination that would be. Who was it who said that youth was wasted on the young?'

'Bernard Shaw,' Alison replied automatically, remembering at the same time her student days when she first became aware of sex. She recalled the terror of thinking she must have conceived after a petting session on a dark sofa; the agony of ignorance and guilt. She began to understand what Clem meant.

'To be young again without a conscience, you mean.'

'That too. The young don't have consciences like we did. The state has taken them over along with teeth and education. They do what they want to do in an open healthy sort of way. We didn't do what we wanted to do and suffered hell for just wanting.'

Alison laughed. 'If you really want that sort of freedom, surely it's not too late.'

Clem was forty-two, three years older than herself and beautiful in a spreading sort of way.

'Of course it's too late. We're the sick generation. Who wants us? Only the young matter, not only to themselves but to the majority of our generation too. The pity of it is that in spite of their free bodies, free minds and consciences, we're the age group that most appreciates freedom.' She sat down on a tin box covered with a tartan rug and lit a cigarette. 'Look at it this way. When we were twenty, we were far too busy husband-seeking and nest-building to think about freedom. In our thirties we were busy bringing up children or trying to make a mark in the world, however ineffectual. Now that we're middle-aged the children don't need us; we no longer care about changing the world. We've entered a sort of second adolescence and we've got to make the most of it. The next stage is senility.'

'So you've got a second chance. What would you do with it?' Alison asked, half amused, half interested.

'Oh – go to the Bahamas and have sex with a bronzed young god on a sun-drenched beach under the spreading palm trees.'

Alison laughed. 'You sound like a travel brochure. There's nothing to stop you if that's what you really want.'

Clem was rich enough to indulge any whim.

'Apart from Honey who would be jealous as hell,' said Clem, laughing and hugging the struggling dog. 'Who'd look at me with all that youth cluttering up the beaches with their slim bikinied bodies? Who'd look at either of us, if it came to that? Tell me honestly, Alison, when did a man last look at you in a randy way?'

Alison considered. There had been a time in her early married life when she had been fully aware of the admiration of other men. She had never been unfaithful, but in the rare months between pregnancies there had been times when all that was required from her was a raised finger. Every year until she had reached the age of thirty or thereabouts, there had been someone. Since then there had been no time and she had not cared.

She looked up and caught a glimpse of herself in the small wall mirror above the dressing table. The poor light and spotty glass made her seem about twenty-five, pretty with soft fair hair and dark blue eyes. She knew she still looked young for her age, but not that young. Perhaps she was incapable of seeing herself as she really was. To herself, she would probably remain twenty-five for ever. She wondered what she looked like to Clem or Ken. She wondered if Ken ever saw her at all. 'I don't remember,' she said, turning away from her reflection, 'and quite honestly I don't care. I couldn't be bothered to fall in love.'

'Who said anything about love?' Clem asked, stuffing a stack of old girlie magazines into the rubbish sack. 'Vicarious sex,' she said, giving them a shove. 'How sick to death one gets of it all. I just think it would be a pleasant change to have a go at the real thing just once more. I can't think of nothing more morale-boosting than to have a man want you for your body alone, to be the apple of someone else's eye for a change. I get so bloody sick of being my own apple.'

'I suppose I'm lucky,' said Alison smugly, 'I've got five apples.'

'Don't deceive yourself,' said Clem seriously. 'Your sons don't need you now. They've flown from the nest and left you stranded. You're in the past tense to them now. They're way ahead of you facing their own futures.'

It was true and in her heart Alison knew it. She had a mental image of five backs turned to her, five pairs of ears stopped to her voice. They were laughing and free. She was free too, but for the life of her she did not know how she was going to live without her chains.

'By the way,' Clem said later when they were drinking tea in the kitchen, 'before I forget the reason why I called in the first place, I'd better break the news. I'm most frightfully sorry but I won't be able to come with you to the city next week. Honey's to be married on Wednesday and that's the day of your meeting, isn't it?'

'Then I shan't go either,' said Alison with relief. 'I was never all that keen to go in the first place.'

'But darling, you must go!' Clem looked at her in consternation. 'I've a list a yard long for Marks and Mary is counting on getting all the village gossip. I promised her you would go.'

Mary was Clem's married sister. Alison had been at school with her and she and Ken always stayed with her on their rare visits to Pendale. 'Besides, it will do you good. You need a break,' Clem added. 'You know how exhausted you always are at the end of the holidays.'

They were still arguing when Ken came in with *The Times* and a can of paraffin for the study stove.

'Ken,' Clem appealed to him. 'Tell Alison she's got to go to the city next week on her own if necessary.'

'Of course she must go,' he said, taking the tea Alison had poured for him. 'You allowed yourself to be elected on to the Diocesan General Purposes Committee on the understanding that you would attend twice a year, didn't you?' he asked his wife.

She nodded.

'Then there's no more to be said, surely. The Dean will give you a lift, weather permitting. He told me he would be going south in an empty car.'

'Big deal,' said Alison into the dregs of her cup. She looked so like her youngest son that Clem had to laugh.

'He must be crazy taking his car through the mountains at this time of the year. I wouldn't risk it,' she said, tapping a sweetener into her second cup.

'It's a great deal cheaper,' said Ken practically.

2

Two days later there was a letter from her youngest son in the morning post. She opened it nervously afraid of finding it full of unhappiness, and started to read:

Dear Mum and Dad,

Thanks for the toffee. It was super. Could you send my new L.P. – the one I got for Christmas because there's a swine here called Biggs who won't let any of the new boys hear his one. Don't throw out my cider. It has to mature for three months at least. We played rugger yesterday and the prefect shouted at the new boys all the time. By the way can I learn the trombone? You get it free the first term . . . P.S. Matron says you forgot my nametapes. P.P.S. It's OK here so far. I hope you are OK.

Although she searched for evidence of unhappiness between the lines, Alison could find none. It was a very different letter from her first convent-supervised letter home, which was not surprising considering how different their childhoods had been. She still regarded her five sons as some kind of miracle.

Being a person who lived very much in the present she had not prepared herself for life without all her children. For weeks now she had been totally involved with Christmas holidays, parties, entertainments and the chores connected with catering for a household of seven. Suddenly it had come to an end, become part of the past, and the present was as solitary and lonely as her childhood and adolescence had been. She had a very real fear of loneliness and her desperation to escape from it now was almost as strong as her desperation to escape from her childhood had once been. Just as she had seen no real hope of escape then, so she did not believe she could escape now. It was almost as if all those years of bringing up her sons had never happened, at least not to the essential Alison. The real Alison was still the lonely child in the big house. She had never really escaped.

It was not that she had had an unhappy childhood. Loneliness and unhappiness were not in her case entirely synonymous. The only child of elderly parents, she lived in a decaying country house, four miles from the nearest village. Here she spent all her childhood and that part of her adolescence which had not been spent in an equally remote Anglican convent school. Her nearest neighbours were her father's sisters, two unmarried women who lived in the dower house at the foot of the long weedy avenue. To call them maiden ladies was misleading for with their cropped grey hair, rough country complexions and odd assortment of dungarees, berets and burberries, they looked more like farm labourers. They ran the estate, such as it was, for their recluse of a brother and were responsible for the dogs, poultry, hedges and gardens. Behind their bluff crisp manner, they were kind, but hardly congenial companions for a diffident schoolgirl.

As she grew older, Alison began to dread the holidays as her school friends dreaded the beginning of term. One of the aunts would meet her at the station, never two at a time for their carefully timed tasks would not permit it. One minute she would be laughing and chattering in the compartment reserved for the school, and the next she would be sitting in the box-shaped bone-shaking car in silence while her aunt would peer short-sightedly at the road ahead, occasionally cursing the other drivers.

After a meal she would change into her holiday clothes which were invariably too tight and too short. She would mooch about her room, read or go for a walk on the moors above the house. It was during these walks that she came alive, for she wove for herself fantastic daydreams in which she was always the centre of a group of adoring brothers, who, as she grew older, easily converted into romantic lovers. In her dreams she was always demonstrative, witty, and completely at ease with the debonair products of her imagination. In fact, she was unusually shy and unforthcoming.

She knew no boys at all, and the only time she had to cope with one of her own age turned out to be a humiliating failure.

An old friend of her mother had called one hot summer afternoon bringing her public-school son. After they had all been sitting in deck chairs in the shade of the rhododendron bushes for a while, her mother suggested she take the boy off on her own.

'Why don't you two go for a walk? It must be so dull for you both listening to all this grown-up chatter.'

The boy's mother smiled her approval and even the aunts acceded with brisk nods, but the boy had scowled. He was too old to be told to go off and play. So was she. They walked in stiff silence under the green canopy of summer trees. Knowing that he had not wanted to come and that it was her mother who had suggested the walk, made her silent with embarrassment. He slouched beside her, kicking at anything which lay in his path. After a while he said:

'Shall we talk about sex?'

She had turned scarlet, unable to answer him because she simply did not know what to say.

He looked at her with disgust on his pink spotty face and drawled, 'Oh, God, don't tell me you're a prude.'

They had walked back to the others in silence and when her mother rose to get the tea things, she had followed her thankfully.

It had not occurred to her that the boy had been rude, only that she had been inadequate. Apart from him she knew no other boys for she did not count the neighbouring farmer's son, a gangling youth in his twenties, who spoke unintelligibly from having lost all but one of his front teeth.

The only other people to play an important role in her life were the local clergymen. It had always been understood within the family that her father would have been ordained if he had not inherited the family estate. He and his sister and to a lesser extent his delicate wife were passionate members of the Anglo-Catholic Church. The sisters filled their house with shrines and bells and holy water stoups. They sang in the choir, cleaned the brasses, ran the various organisations including the Mothers' Union. They attended every service provided, week-day and Sunday. Her father read the lessons and, as patron of three village churches, took a paternal interest in his rectors. Alison was expected to share the general fervour. At an early age she was inoculated with religion with the result that she never really caught it. On the other hand, it was as much a part of her as the pigmentation under her skin. She neither questioned nor argued the truth of what she was told, and it was not until years later that it occurred to her to doubt any of the doctrines. She took it all for granted. Church on Sunday was one of the high spots of the holidays, and the only other events of consequence were the frequent visits of the clergy.

There was one she remembered – a particular favourite with her aunts because of his celibacy – who used to ride a woman's bicycle with a skirt guard to protect his cassock. Another – a favourite of hers – had converted the top floor of his rectory into a railway lay-out. On rare occasions she was invited to watch the trains in operation, and once was allowed to work the controls. There was one whose flamboyant gestures and flowery pulpit language fascinated her. She was sure he would fall out of the pulpit, a high box affair with a creaking inadequate rail. He grew enormous strawberries and once she was allowed loose under the net, a treat never granted to her by the aunts in her own garden.

Whatever their virtues or inadequacies they were kind to her and she had liked them all, even the one who left in a hurry for some awful undisclosed reason. Some she had loved. As a breed she found them gentle and unpretentious. It was not surprising therefore that she had married one.

For a long time she did not believe she would marry at all. She did not think there could be any other life for her away from the crumbling house and the little churches. She had a vague idea of herself growing old and coarse in feature like her aunts, tending first her aged relations and then finally the house until both she and it crumbled away from age and decay. She was not able to visualise a future for herself in any other environment. She would continue to help her aunts with their jigsaw puzzles and their stamp collecting; fish or play croquet with her father, cook and sew with her mother, her life one long uneventful holiday of loneliness.

As she had never visualised escape for herself, when it came in the form of a place at university, she never quite believed it was intended for her. She was also a little afraid of it. Perhaps her marriage to Ken had been a compromise between the old secure existence and the bewildering new one. Even when she was married and her sons were little boys, she never really believed that it had all happened to the same person who had lived such a solitary childhood. The day would come when she would find herself alone again. She would wake up and find it had all been a dream. It seemed now that perhaps that day had come. The boys, having gone, might never have existed outside her imagination. Even the letter in her hand was only a scrap of paper torn from an exercise book.

She still had Ken, of course, but in some ways Ken's presence seemed to increase her loneliness. It was as if he stood in the same relationship to her now as her father had stood when she was a child. More and more he reminded her of her father, and increasingly he appeared to play the same role in her mature life as her father had played all those years ago. Just as she had loved her father, so she loved Ken, deeply, but without too much involvement.

A tutor in Psychology at university had once told her that she had fallen in love with Ken because he had represented a special sort of security in the shape of God-the-Father. Similarly he told her that Ken had fallen in love with her for she had represented to him innocence in the form of the Madonna. He had said that their marriage could not last for the one could not live in intimacy with the Virgin Mary any more than the other could sleep with God. As soon as each realised the other was human, the crash would come. The psychologist had been wrong, but partly because she had been too busy with babies and he with trying to cope with parish affairs to become too involved with each other's inadequacies. They had not had time to look for feet of clay.

They met, appropriately enough, in church. The sun had lain like a halo on her long fair hair and she had caught and held his rapt look. She had known then that he was the man she would marry. Even though she was in love with another man at the time, she knew she would marry this stranger on leave as a Naval Chaplain. She had not hurried the courtship; she had not even waited behind after the service to be introduced. Sooner or later they would meet. In a queer way she was sorry it had happened so soon. At eighteen, she felt she was too young to marry.

Her parents, if not overjoyed at the prospect of a penniless son-in-law, accepted him into the family with grace, and the two aunts heard of the engagement with tight smiles that hinted approval.

Although Ken was not the sort of man to speak much about love, Alison was confident that his affection was as strong as hers. The whole affair had such an element of destiny about it that one of the aunts was heard to say at the wedding that if ever a marriage were made in heaven this was it.

It was a high-flown beginning to what was to become a very down-to-earth marriage which Alison learned to take in her stride and to which Ken, who was by nature solitary, did his best to adapt.

After a short spell in the Navy and some hectic years in the centre of an industrial town, he brought his family to the peace and safety of village life. Alison, a countrywoman by birth and inclination, immediately loved the small community which in some ways seemed no more than an extension of her own family, and was happy enough with her children in the huge unhandy parsonage by the sea.

But Ken was as little a countryman as he had been city dweller. He was a man who lived in a world apart and within. After twenty years of marriage, Alison still could not gauge his inner thoughts and feelings. Their marriage was non-communicative but not, she thought, from boredom or lack of love, but rather from the nature of his own personality. A deep inner reserve combined with an outer shyness of manner made him a difficult man to know. Intellectual and intelligent, he spent a great deal of time in his study writing or researching for his book on the doctrines of the Celtic Church, a world from which she was excluded.

And yet, she thought, it was by no means an unsuccessful marriage. Had she been of a possessive nature, she could have made his life a torment, for there were large areas he was unable and unwilling to share. Fortunately for him she had no time to be possessive. In her rare moments of peace when the children had been younger, she did not have the energy to try to penetrate her husband's heart. They took each other for granted, and she relied on him as on her own right hand, and he had not let her down. Although she had assumed the major share of the upbringing of their sons, he had been there to help with the big decisions and to rebuke the major offences. The boys obeyed him on the rare occasions when he insisted on absolute obedience without argument, out of respect.

Alison's love was bounded by a similar respect. She respected him for maintaining the principles she was too lazy to uphold. She respected him for his profession and his loyalty to all its rules and demands. His quiet intellectual sermons pleased her, and the amount of time he spent in prayer impressed her, for, apart from involuntary ejaculaions in times of stress, she had not prayed properly for years. She admired him for the hours he spent in the chilly little church. She had the feeling that it did not much matter what she did or how she thought, provided Ken still maintained the standards with which they had both started. She kept up a pretence by going to most of his services, and by organising church activities among the women. As long as he led the good life, it did not really matter what she did. She had the feeling that if he were to lose his faith or fall below his own high standards, the results would be disastrous for them both. Deep down she thought that the virgin birth, the Resurrection and Judgement Day were as mythical as the tales of Zeus and Apollo. On the other hand she could be wrong and she wanted, above all, Ken to be on the safe side. She believed that she could cope with Hell, whatever that might be, but she did not want Ken to have to try. She preferred him to remain encapsulated against loss of faith, lack of love, the world, the flesh and the devil, like a spaceman on the moon.

Therefore she did not argue when he insisted that it was her duty to go to Pendale, although she had neither the energy nor the inclination to attend the meeting. When the actual day came, she packed her overnight bag without enthusiasm. The first week without her sons had been longer and drearier than any other she could remember. Ken had been particularly engrossed in his work. He did not seem to notice the long silences broken only by the creaking of old boards which expanded and contracted in the January frosts. A creeping chill seemed to emanate from the empty attic rooms and for the first few days she had been intensely miserable.

She knew she ought to do something constructive with her time. Now was the chance to develop a new hobby, study a language or a period in history (how surprised Ken would be), take up weaving or basketwork. She could even indulge that suspected talent for painting; she could decorate the drawing-room. Heaven knew it needed it. Yet

23

every suggestion bored her. She reviewed the list of village activities, drama, choir, institute and dismissed them all as impossibly dreary.

A trip to the city would do her good, as Clem so practically put it. Yet, if she had her choice, she would have cancelled the trip. The thought of the meetings filled her with horror. At heart, she cared not at all for the work of the Welfare Committee which consisted of do-gooders, both clerical and lay, from all over the diocese. When she had accepted the nomination, she had thought that it would be a good excuse for a free jaunt to the city and a couple of days' window-shopping.

It was a bore having to go with the Dean. Admittedly, she hardly knew him, but what she had heard was not prepossessing. He was respected as a good preacher and committee-man, but disliked for dogmatic views and an unapproachable manner. Of all the clergy in the diocese he was the last she would have chosen as a travelling companion. If only Ken would come too and share the burden of conversation, but when she had suggested it, he had refused to consider the idea.

'But why, darling?' she had argued. 'You know you could do with a break. Now that the boys are all away, there's no reason why we should not have a couple of days away together.'

'I have a great deal to prepare for Lent, and the proofs of my book need correcting this week,' he said decisively.

She was still annoyed. She knew that he did not want to go. He enjoyed the stillness of the vicarage and would enjoy it even more on his own for a couple of days. She knew this and did not resent it, normally. She too enjoyed occasional days without him. She supposed most marriages gained strength from occasional private retreats, but in her restless

24

unhappy state of mind she did not see why he should not, for once, make an effort to please her. It had often been a cause of dissent between them, this dislike of his for any form of social activity. Holidays, parties, particularly drink parties, bored him, and the longer he lived, the less reason he saw for accepting invitations. She had learned not to press him, and in time the villagers learned not to invite him, but this was different.

'I don't see why you won't come,' she nagged, and again, 'please, dear, it would be fun for both of us.'

He refused to change his mind, and later, in the light of what was to happen, she wondered whether, subconsciously, she had pressed him so hard to give her the excuse she needed for what she was about to do.

Instead he gave her some extra money that they could not afford and with that she had to be content.

He drove her to the hotel in the busy market town of Cool-water Bay, the Rural Dean's parish, where he had arranged with Ken to meet her. They said little on the journey for she was still annoyed with him, unreasonably so, and she knew it, but she was not able to stop that secret flow of bile. She said no more, however, for she had long ago learned that in a spoken quarrel with Ken, she was the one who said too much and therefore she was the one who got hurt. Instead she watched the sea from the window. It was a grey world, grey sea under grey clouds, grey fields, grey sheep and grey gulls. They matched her mood.

3

The Dean arrived on the stroke of the hour as Ken had predicted. As always he gave Alison an impression of obstinacy and conscious superiority. Such persons, she usually found, tended to be little men asking to be deflated, but not the Dean.

Big-boned, with long heavy limbs and jutting features in a furrowed face, George Tindall, Rural Dean of the Diocese of Pendale and Vicar of Coolwater Bay, inspired awe rather than affection. His head like his other features was larger than average and his heavily lined brow receded into a stiff brush of grey hair. He wore glasses which continually caught the light thus effectively hiding his rather fine grey eyes. Whereas Ken in a soft collar could be anything from a gentle school-master to a mild little office clerk, the Dean could be none other than what he was, an uncompromising minister of religion. She had never known him to smile.

After dealing with her case, Ken and he stood for a minute in the car-park and exchanged a few remarks in the manner of men who respect each other enough not to need small talk. Neither of them included her in their conversation by a glance, let alone a remark. The Dean did not so much as turn his head to acknowledge her greeting. Humiliated to the point of anger, she got into the car which was the same make as her own, though the gleaming paintwork and tidy interior made it seem a new model compared with the slum of mud and crisp papers that hers became during the holidays.

'Put on your safety belt,' the Dean said at length when he had climbed into the driver's seat.

He made her feel like a piece of baggage that he had promised somewhat grudgingly to deliver. She supposed he must have offered her the lift out of Christian charity but she wished it would extend to making her feel less of a liability. As they drove through the outskirts of the town she found herself remembering the conversation she had had with Clem on the day the boys left home. How right Clem had been. She did not think she could make this man notice her if she were to spend the rest of the journey doing a strip-tease. The comparison between the Dean's imperviousness to her as a woman as set against her somewhat rusty powers to attract was an amusing speculation. Although she did not think she stood a chance of winning from him so much as a smile, it would be an intriguing occupation for the journey and a laughing point for herself and Clem in the weeks to come if she were to try. He was, she felt, fair game.

At the same time she was aware that it would give her extreme pleasure to be able to make him turn his great head and look at her with something approaching interest. The improbability of such an event made her smile and she began to feel better. For the first time since the end of the holidays, the boys receded from the immediate conscious of her mind and she relaxed. The lengthening silence in the car did not trouble her. It was at least as much the Dean's responsibility to speak as it was hers. She could wait. Having come to this decision she turned to look out of the window.

It was beautiful. The big car climbed easily up into the hills. All round, the mountains, brown-backed and bony, stretched their white tips to the January sky. Now that she had got over the hurdle of leaving home, she found herself actually glad she had come. She felt a sense of freedom coupled with extreme physical well-being. She was one of the lucky women; she had thrived on making her sons. Child-bearing had given her an athlete's body. Her legs were strong and well-shaped, her hips wide but thinly fleshed, her belly flat and her back supple. Only her breasts, criss-crossed by silver stretch marks, bore evidence of her maternity. She was surprised that she should suddenly be so aware of her body. It was something she had taken for granted for so long that she had ceased to regard it as anything other than functional. Now for the first time in years she felt she might still be attractive and she felt a growing confidence that in her present mood she could make any man, even this man, respond to her.

He was the first to speak. Engrossed in her thoughts, she did not realise that the silence had grown oppressive until, turning to answer his question, she saw a film of sweat on his forehead. It was at that moment that it occurred to her for the first time that he might not be the man he seemed.

He was asking her about her sons.

Leaning back, she answered at length, giving each child a fair amount of attention in her reply. She was aware that she was over-answering what was merely a conventional question, but there was something in his tone that told her that he was intrigued by the fact of her motherhood. When she had finished she looked at him and smiled, deliberately determined to charm him.

'You should know better than to ask a mother about her sons.'

He frowned slightly but did not reply. She remembered then that he and his wife had no children and she wondered

28

if he minded. It was a question she would normally have asked only a close friend, but in her present mood she did not care what she said to him. On the other hand, it was not entirely a casual question. She was interested.

'Do you mind not having a son?' she asked softly.

As she spoke, part of her stood back in amazement at the uncharacteristic provocation in her voice. The interior of the car had become as intimate as a bedroom. Although he made no reply, his hand seemed to shake as he lifted it off the steering wheel to change gear.

'I'm sorry,' she said falsely, 'perhaps I shouldn't have asked.'

Her quiet apology seemed to increase his tension. She was astonished at her power to disturb him and was tempted to disbelieve her assessment of the situation until she saw the sweat mark on the gear lever. She knew she ought to let the subject drop, but she could not leave it alone. Part of her, the intrigued female part, wanted to probe a little deeper.

'I have the feeling you don't particularly like children – or women either . . .'

'Like – mind – feel,' he said harshly. 'Emotions are not that important.'

Normally such a remark would have daunted her, but not on this occasion. It made him a more worthwhile opponent in what had suddenly become a battle. She stirred in her seat, enjoying the play. They were well-matched for both were able to take care of themselves, or so it seemed to her. But she did not look for victory. It was the contest she enjoyed.

'But how dull life would be without them,' she replied easily.

They climbed deeper into the mountains. The peaks

and mounds had torn holes in the blanket of cloud to reveal patches of dazzling blue sky. As the car followed the course of a dale, the sun came out silvering the slender birches that lined the road. Beyond the birch glade an old stone bridge thickly covered with moss spanned an untidy boulder-strewn stream. Beyond the bridge a rough track led over the moors and lost itself in a desolation of hills. In past journeys to Pendale, she had often noticed the bridge and wondered where the lonely track could lead. Her family laughed at her romantic speculations, but to her it was not only the prettiest part of the journey but also the most mysterious.

'I've always wanted to cross that bridge and see where the track leads to,' she said spontaneously, thinking aloud.

She was so used to her family ignoring such a remark that she was surprised when the Dean drew into a convenient lay-by and pulled on the hand-brake.

'Why not?' he said.

She looked at him in astonishment. 'What about the meeting? It starts at two-thirty, doesn't it?'

'A pity,' he said, faintly contemptuous. 'I thought you meant it.'

'I'm not used to having my whims taken seriously,' she said, 'but yes, I meant it. As you say, why not?'

She opened the door and got out. An icy wind whipped her coat against her legs and stung her eyes. Much as she loved walking, this was neither the day nor the weather to go for a tramp in the hills. She had the feeling she had been out-manœuvred. Round two to the Dean, she thought with a shiver as she waited for him to lock the car. If he dawdled she would capitulate.

But he did not dawdle. His black raincoat flapped against his body and it took her all her time to keep abreast of him. When they reached the bridge, they stopped for a moment to catch their breath. Her lungs ached from the ice in the wind.

'Look,' he said suddenly. 'Can you see them?'

She could see nothing.

'Deer. There must be at least two dozen.'

Still she could not see them. He came close to her and pointed to the snow-line. She sensed his excitement. Then she saw what looked like a string of boulders far above them. One of them moved.

'How on earth did you spot them?' she asked, impressed.

'A matter of knowing what to look for.'

She noticed that his grey complexion was tinged with colour and the stern line of his mouth had relaxed.

'We'll see how close we can get to them before they get wind of us.'

He turned and without waiting to see if she were following, led the way up the rough track over the hill.

At first she thought she would have to give up. He was already yards ahead of her and walking easily over the rough ground. But presently the stitch in her side eased, and her breath ceased to saw her lungs. Her body began to glow with the exercise and she no longer cared about the state of her long boots.

After a steep trudge they reached the summit of one of the lesser foothills. All round them the mountains reared like breasts snow-nippled to the sky. The Dean shaded his eyes.

'There they go!' he said, pointing to the snow-line.

But she was not looking at the deer. The track which they had followed continued for several hundred yards further over the brow of the hill and ended in a ruin of stones that had obviously once been a dwelling of some size. Well off the road and hidden from all other signs of human habitation, the loneliness of the site must have been appalling. No human being could have lived for long surrounded by such splendid desolation.

The sight of the ruins depressed her. The track which in her imagination had promised a fairy-tale ending had led to nothing, worse than nothing. In some ways it was ominous, though she could not tell why she should think so.

A round cloud, the colour of tar-smoke, obliterated the sun and hurled a fistful of fine snow in their faces. They both turned automatically to go back to the car.

After the first steep moments of descent, the rest was easy, and by the time they reached the car she had forgotten her depression and felt warm and full of well-being. The windows misted with their breathing, and when he took off his glasses to wipe them, his eyes were clear and benign.

'That was marvellous,' she said, turning to him eagerly. 'I'm glad you made me do it.'

'That's not quite how I would have put it,' he said drily, and inserted the ignition key.

'Let's eat now,' she said quickly. 'I don't know about you, but I'm starving.'

She reached behind for her shopping bag and after spreading a cloth over her knees, took out a paper bag stuffed with new rolls, a packet of butter and thick slices of cold ham wrapped in greaseproof paper. The floury rolls rasped slightly between her fingers as she spread them, and the car smelled of new bread. The Dean produced a plastic container filled with pale crustless triangles of bread threaded faintly with pink paste.

She knew enough of the Dean's wife to guess that these anaemic morsels were of her construction. The genteel pillar of a parson's wife with her clipped and careful tongue, weak handshake and restrained tea-party smile had long ago earned Alison's dislike by an overheard comment to do with clergy wives who bred like rabbits. On the few occasions they had met, Joan Tindall had been something more than superior and less than civil. There were plenty of women who fluttered like maiden aunts at Alison's fecundity. Others were afraid of it. She sensed that the Dean's wife was disgusted. Alison could pity her, but she could not help wondering why the Dean, or any other man for that matter, had married her.

She handed him a roll thick with ham and butter and knew that he would eat at least three. Nor did he refuse the beaker of hot soup she poured from her own flask. But she felt ashamed of her small surge of triumph when he returned Joan's container to the pigeon hole in the dashboard, untouched. She was not at war with the Dean's wife.

'That derelict house up there,' she said when the edge of their appetite had been blunted. 'I reckon it must have been built by a saint or a lunatic.'

'You are partly right.'

She turned to him in surprise.

'Do you know the story then?'

'It's well enough known in these parts.'

She asked him to tell her about it.

'Over a hundred years ago, the daughter of a local squire fell in love with a labourer. It caused a great scandal, as the result of which the girl lost her reason. Rather than shut her up in the nearest Bedlam, her father built a house for her in the remotest part of his estate and paid a retainer to take care of her.'

'How cruel,' Alison said. 'Why couldn't the poor girl love her labourer? Her madness was probably no more than a broken heart.'

'You prejudge the issue,' he said. 'The labourer was already married with half a dozen children of his own and the girl was crazy enough to try to kill her keeper.'

'And the moralists would say it all happened because she had sinned.'

When he did not immediately reply she added, deliberately out to taunt him, 'And no doubt you would agree with them?'

'Suppositions such as that are as time-wasting in the asking as they are in the answering,' he replied shortly, snapping the thin cord of affinity she had tried to thread round them. Glancing at him swiftly, she saw that his skin had lost its colour and that he had begun to sweat again. She wondered if he were not well. Presently he opened the car door and went outside for a few minutes. While he was away she loosened her coat and began to brush her hair which, in spite of a head-scarf, had become tangled and untidy. She pulled down the sun-shade above the windscreen which had a mirror set in it and looked at her reflection critically. Her cheeks were still glowing from the wind and her eyes had a bright almost hectic gleam. As she brushed and adjusted her hair, she had the feeling she was looking at a stranger.

She was still brushing her hair when the Dean returned. His glasses glinted as he glanced swiftly at her. Sensing doubtful approval, she put away her brush with a small smile. It was the first time he had looked at her with intent all morning. Her smile broadened and she turned her head away so that he should not be aware of her amusement. She was not laughing at him, however, but at herself for being so ridiculous as to think she could flirt with him. Silly word, she thought, biting her curling lip. Silly creature. She imagined her sons' humourless horror at the thought of their mother making a pass at a man. Pull yourself together, she told herself. Be your age. But she was enjoying herself. It had been a long time since she had enjoyed herself in such a totally irresponsible way.

With an effort of will she forced the smile off her face and into the back of her mind. She began to question him sensibly on the subject of climbing and was surprised to find how much he knew about it. It had been the passion of his youth and he knew the names and points of interest of all the peaks in the area. Although he spoke well and with knowledge, she was more interested in his animation than in his subject-matter. Two red spots appeared high on his cheeks as he spoke of corries and crampons, scree and crevasses. He was a different man and she played deliberately to the difference by feeding him with questions and interest.

Soon the car had passed through the mountains and was descending between the rounded grassy foothills. They reminded her of the long lonely walks of her childhood and how she used to cling close to the little bright streams for company.

'I'm afraid of mountains,' she told him after a while.

'Afraid?' he repeated, surprised.

'Perhaps it was the mountains that drove that poor girl mad.'

'What girl?' He had forgotten the story he had told her earlier until she reminded him.

'Nonsense,' he said scornfully.

'Why is it nonsense?' She turned to him, her voice soft and curious. 'Most people have fears, don't they? I'm afraid of empty houses, dark rooms, dentists, earwigs, cancer, as well as mountains and a hundred and one things for my children. I couldn't begin to tell you.'

He took his eyes off the road to look at her and she caught the quick gleam of something sad.

'You don't know the meaning of fear,' he said quietly.

The tension between them was almost visible, a sunbeam trapped with dust. The spots of colour had gone from his cheeks and his skin had a greasy sheen of uneasiness. She knew then that it was fear that made him sweat, in comparison with which her own dreads were of little account.

'What are you afraid of?' she asked so gently that when he did not reply she thought that perhaps he had not heard.

'What is there to be afraid of?' she repeated the question in the same soft curious tone.

'For God's sake,' he said roughly, 'leave me alone.'

'I'm sorry,' she told him gently.

He did not accept or reject her apology but continued to watch the road ahead with a grim unhappy expression. She wondered briefly if he were afraid of her, but dismissed the idea as ludicrous.

Yawning suddenly, she realised that the walk and the strong air had made her sleepy. She closed her eyes and dozed.

She dreamed about her sons. They were driving towards her in her eldest son's van. Their faces, detached from their bodies, looked vaguely like the paintings of the five winged cherubs. Ranged behind the windscreen they stared past her with sad unseeing eyes. Trying to attract their attention, she moved into the path of the van and waved her arms. To avoid her the van skidded and swerved off the road. At the same time she awoke. The noise and her terror were so real that she thought she must have cried out. When she opened her eyes she saw that they had reached the dual carriageway on the outskirts of Pendale. The car was passing a transporter and the noise had been part of her dream. She closed her eyes again and her imagination took over where her dream had left off. The van plunged over an enbank-

36

ment. She saw the broken bodies of her sons strewn across the road. Her breasts ached and she was aware of a familiar yearning pain that often filled her when she thought about her children.

She had first felt the ache as a child during the long nights at school away from home. A sweet sad sickness that she could only describe as a yearning for familiar faces. She had experienced the same feeling when she had held her first son to her breast and felt him draw the milk. With each of her subsequent children the yearning grew stronger and combined with such an ache in her womb that she sometimes cried out loud. She knew that, physically, her womb was contracting after the stretch of pregnancy, but she often wondered if her body still yearned for the child it had expelled. She had heard of hearts contracting with love. With her it was the womb. Sometimes she wondered if the source of female emotion lay in the womb. She believed that it could be so, for it had given her the deepest pleasure and the most exquisite pain.

In latter years she had felt the same yearning contraction when any of her children had been suffering or unhappy. Most recently she had felt it as she stood on the station platform and waved goodbye to her youngest son.

Thrusting her hands into the deep pockets of her coat, she pressed her fingers against her lower stomach. The pain and the anguish were indivisible. Firmly she told herself that her sons were well, her husband was well. There was no logical cause for this inexplicable inner panic.

She turned to her companion for comfort with some trite remark on her lips, but his grim expression was so unreassuring that she looked away again, the words unspoken.

37

4

They were nearly an hour late for the meeting. The Dean took his place near the top of the long polished table and opened his brief-case while the Convener filled him in on what had already been said.

There was a spare chair at the foot of the table which Alison was about to take when one of the few women present patted a seat next to her and whispered without an apparent glimmer of humour:

'Friend, move up higher.'

She was a vast woman extravagantly dressed in vivid colours with a startling crimson velvet hat.

'I saw your name on the list of committee members and hoped you would come. We've met before; do you remember?'

Alison was not likely to forget. Mrs Gerber-Hythe had once attended a 'Quiet Day' for women, dressed dramatically from head to foot in black and wearing a rusty lace mantilla. Even the austere reverend father conducting the proceedings was put off his stride.

'My dear, we'll talk later, but just now I want to have my little say.'

She stood up in a flurry of scarves and perfume. She was like a butterfly in a nest of houseflies and it was obvious both clergy and laity adored her. She spoke at some length about an isolated country charge where she had found the vicar to be 'quite charming'. No one present at the meeting saw the relevance of her story, but everyone enjoyed listening. Mrs Gerber-Hythe was on a number of diocesan committees partly because she was willing to give the necessary time, partly because her mild eccentricities lightened the normally dull agenda, and partly because she never found even the dreariest of the clergy anything less than charming. It was a relief for the fathers to find such unshakeable loyalty. Her devotion extended also to the wives and showed itself not only in words but in countless small and not so small deeds known only to herself and those families she helped. Mrs Gerber-Hythe was a rich woman in all senses of the word.

'And now, my dear, I'm sure you agree with me,' she whispered to Alison as she sat down again.

Alison smiled. 'I would agree with you if you said you lived on Mars and attended Mattins on Venus,' she whispered softly, not to interrupt the new speaker.

'Naughty, but I like you.'

Alison looked up smiling and caught the glint of the Dean's spectacles from the far end of the table. She knew that he was looking at her, but she could not read his expression. Sensing his disapproval she felt faintly depressed. It occurred to her with surprise that she cared for his opinion. His approval mattered to her. There had been a time in her youth when she wanted the approval of everyone she met. She had long since grown out of that immature phase. The approval or disapproval of acquaintances was something she no longer considered. What did it matter, she asked herself, what the Dean thought of her, and yet incredibly it did matter. His good opinion of her was of greater importance that what she thought about him.

She looked away determined to concentrate sensibly on

the discussion which was now centred on the Church's policy towards Mission in general. An intelligent-looking young priest was speaking.

'The Christian Gospel is about humanity and I believe that our job – as missionaries if you like – is to help each other grow into our full potential as human beings.'

'Surely the Christian Gospel is something over and above mere humanity,' said Martin Sharpe pompously.

Martin was a college contemporary of Ken and no one knew how he managed to insinuate himself on to every available diocesan committee, for he was a long-winded bore who antagonised his listeners by a patronising manner combined with a Heep-like humility. Listening to him made Alison shrink.

'You are wrong,' said the Dean shortly. 'Christianity is not something over and above humanity. How could it be? Christianity is humanity in its highest form and Mission is the recognition of Christ in every individual.'

Martin Sharpe flushed, for the Dean's tone had been as insolent as his words were enlightened. Alison's fists tightened in her lap.

'In my experience,' Martin began patronisingly, 'Christians are as little interested in humanity as they are in Mission. Our job as vicars is to encourage the laity to support us and enable us to be better priests, and I am happy to report that as a result of a little experiment . . .'

'Nonsense,' the Dean interrupted rudely. 'Our job is to help the laity to do their own jobs better – not ours.'

Martin Sharpe tilted back his chair. 'You can't be serious,' he said with a heavy attempt at humour. 'What you are virtually saying is that we should train the laity to be better soldiers, sailors and candlestick makers.'

He looked round but failed to catch a single eye.

40

' "Train" is not a word in my vocabulary, Sharpe, though I imagine it features frequently in yours. The Church's job is to encourage your plumbers, your bank-managers, or your Trade Union officials to respect the humanity of the individual in his employment. This is Mission.'

'With the enabling grace of God,' the Convener interposed, anxious to close the antagonistic discussion.

'I would like to ask the Dean one question if you will permit it, Mr Chairman,' Martin Sharpe said with an ingratiating smile, and, without waiting for permission, continued, 'There are not enough professional clergy to man the Sunday services let alone the other sacraments of the Church. How does the Dean imagine we have the time or the resources to instruct businessmen in the skilled art of public relations?'

'Shut half the buildings in this over-churched country – starting with yours, Sharpe!'

Turkey-red with humiliation, Sharpe opened his mouth to demand an apology, not without justification for the Dean's tone had matched his words for insolence. Alison, like the others, held her breath and stared at the table in front of her in embarrassment. She wished Martin Sharpe would sit down and shut up. Fortunately Mrs Gerber-Hythe was too quick for him. Like the hostess at a dinner party she rose majestically and, cutting through Sharpe's protestations, said with a gracious smile that would have done justice to the Queen-Mother:

'Friends, may we adjourn for tea? I happen to know mine has been ready for at least' – she consulted her watch – 'twenty-five minutes.'

The Convener shot to his feet. 'My dear lady, I do apologise. Tea, of course, of course! We will meet again tomorrow at ten.'

Like a flock of blackbirds, the clergy rose to a man and bowed their heads for the Benediction.

'Is there really tea?' Alison asked, collecting her things together.

'My dear, I shouldn't think so. I said the first thing that came into my head.'

Looking at her with admiration, Alison discovered another reason why Mrs Gerber-Hythe was so popular on committees. Peacemakers are rare birds.

'But there is tea at my place. Why don't you come home with me?' she continued, looking down at Alison with a warm smile.

It was a pleasant thought and Alison hesitated, tempted to accept the invitation. Over Mrs Gerber-Hythe's shoulder she could see the Dean being talked to by a diminutive elderly Canon. The Dean looked impatient, irritable and tired.

'Another time, perhaps,' she told her.

'Mrs Osmond, what have you done to that Dean of yours?' One of the diocesan social workers approached her with an outstretched hand. 'I've never known him to be quite so touchy.'

'Sharpe asks for it every time,' said another woman whom Alison recognised as the diocesan youth adviser.

'Even so . . .'

Alison found that she did not have to say anything. The conversation zig-zagged back and forth among the departing members. Everyone was friendly to her and made her feel welcome.

'What time did you start this morning? Did you have a ghastly journey?' she was asked in varying forms by at least half a dozen people.

'They think we in the northern part of the diocese live in

igloos in winter and change to caves for the summer holidays,' she told Mrs Gerber-Hythe as they crossed the hall and walked towards the outer door.

'And don't you?' her companion laughed. 'My dear, if you won't come and see me today, you must come tomorrow.'

'The Dean wants to be back by the early evening.'

'Don't tell me you risked driving through the mountains at this time of the year?'

'Why not?'

'You must be mad.'

'It all ties up with living in caves,' Alison replied, laughing.

'It's the only explanation.' Mrs Gerber-Hythe dropped her voice and took Alison's arm, drawing her aside. 'My dear, I'm really worried about George Tindall. I've known him for years — though when I say "known" him, I exaggerate. He's not a man who allows himself to be known, particularly by women. At the moment I feel he's on the edge of some sort of private volcano.'

'What can I do about it?'

Mrs Gerber-Hythe looked at Alison quickly, surprised by her sharp tone.

'You can be kind to him,' she said.

Alison looked away ashamed. It struck her as odd that Mrs Gerber-Hythe should have used those particular words for there was more significance in them than she could have possibly guessed. Alison had not been kind. Those probing provocative questions which had been intended as a form of self-amusement to while away a dull journey now seemed in retrospect to have been callous.

'Of course,' she said quietly.

She looked up then and saw that the Dean was looking at her across the hall. As soon as he caught her eye, he gestured

43

to her to wait, and without ceremony left the Canon talking to himself. Mrs Gerber-Hythe saw him coming.

'My dear, I must fly. No, I won't wait. I can see George tomorrow. Don't forget what I said.'

She walked towards the door where she was caught by the Canon who was by now thoroughly cross.

'I can't think what some of the clergy are coming to these days. Can't get a civil word out of them.'

Although everyone in the hall must have heard, the Dean gave no sign that he had done so.

'What are your plans?' he asked her, and glanced at his watch.

Shopping, dinner with Jim and Mary, a good long gossip and then bed in Mary's comfortable spare room. It had been planned for days, but she said, 'Nothing in particular.'

'There's a play on at the Queen's – a London preview. I'm told it's amusing. If I can get tickets, would you care to go?'

She was so surprised that for a moment she did not answer. She thought quickly. A telephone call would fix Mary. If she hurried there would be time to catch Marks before it shut. There might even be time to buy a new dress. She had the feeling that although he had made the invitation in good faith, he would not mind if she refused. She decided however to accept.

'Why not?' she said, consciously echoing his reply to her when she had talked about crossing the bridge.

Even without Mrs Gerber-Hythe's exhortation to be kind, she would have accepted.

5

As she walked down the High Street and gazed into the gay shop windows, Alison was in a complacent mood. She admitted freely to herself that she was both flattered and surprised by the Dean's unexpected invitation. She had to smile when she remembered how low she had rated her chances of winning from him so much as a favourable glance, and now this. But her amusement was at her own expense. She was behaving like a schoolgirl asked for her first date.

Being in the mood to buy, she had no difficulty in finding the right dress. It was green, the colour of the rosemary bush in the vicarage garden. It cost more than she had intended to spend and she knew she would have regrets later, but for the moment she was pleased with her buy. Against it, her hair looked like the underpetals of a lesser celandine. One extravagance led to another and when she found it was late-closing in most of the shops, she pandered to her mood of self-indulgence. By the time she reached the hotel near the theatre where she had arranged to meet the Dean, she was as decked with parcels as a Christmas tree.

He was waiting for her in the lounge with a morose expression and she was aware of the gulf between her gaiety and his gloom. Confident that her arrival would be enough to change his mood, she approached, smiling.

'Hullo,' she said, dropping her parcels on an empty chair and hoping he would buy her a drink. 'I've bought a new dress. Do you like it?'

She opened her coat to show him, but he paid no attention.

'You're late,' he said coldly as he stood up and folded the evening paper.

She was about to retort sharply when she noticed that the paper in his hands was shaking. Mrs Gerber-Hythe was right. There was definitely something wrong with him. Remembering her promise to be kind she turned away and began to pick up her parcels.

'Shall we put these in the car?'

'No time,' he replied shortly. He picked up the larger of her paper carriers and walked over to the reception desk. 'We can pick them up later.'

While he was fetching his coat she went to the cloakroom. Brushing her hair had a calming effect. Her mouth curved in a smile as she stared at her reflection in the glass. She was confident she had the power to make him unwind if she cared to use it.

They were, after all, in plenty of time for the play. The theatre, newly decorated, was warm with red plush and gold paint. He had managed to get two cancellations in the front stalls and as she took her seat she felt a pleasurable thrill of anticipation. It was years since she had been to the theatre. To her surprise he had even bought some chocolates.

His large frame overflowed the narrow seat and she leaned away, careful not to touch him. Her fastidiousness was surprising for she was not normally afraid of physical contact. With both men and women friends she enjoyed the comforting feel of an arm or the brush of lips and cheek. She still held hands with her youngest son, provided he was certain no one was watching. Yet for some reason she was very much aware of his black-clad arm on the rest of the seat, and she did not want to touch it.

The play was slick, modern and full of stock situations and minor blasphemies. The audience, mainly young and smart, seemed to be enjoying it, but to her it was no better than a second-rate television comedy half-hour dragged out to four times its acceptable length. I must be getting old, she thought, remembering how indiscriminately she had enjoyed the theatre when she was a student. She wondered what the Dean was making of it.

Out of boredom she resorted to the family habit of finding likenesses between television actors and her friends.

'Why can't you let people be themselves without always looking for their doubles?' Ken would grumble, but he was better than any of them at the game.

One of the characters wearing a red hat entered the stage with a flamboyant sweep of her voluminous skirts.

'Mrs Gerber-Hythe,' Alison said involuntarily.

The Dean stared at her and then turning back to look at the actress began to laugh. The audience immediately around them turned with smiles and their own laughter increased at his evident enjoyment. Even the actors on stage were aware of him and played up accordingly. She had never seen him smile, let alone laugh, and it occurred to her that she was seeing him for the first time, not as he was, but as he might have been, or might yet be.

Presently he took off his glasses and wiped his eyes.

'So you do that too,' she whispered.

'Do what?'

'Cry when you laugh.'

He thought for a moment. 'I suppose I do,' he admitted, surprised.

It occurred to her that if he had not known this simple fact about himself, he could not have been in the habit of laughing. They sat through another scene made bearable

47

by matching characters to members of the diocesan committee.

'What do you think of the play?' he asked at the interval.

'Pretty so-so,' she said, unwilling to condemn it outright in case he should think her ungrateful.

'I agree; it's appalling. Let's go.'

She followed him into the foyer.

'The hotel does a good meal or would you rather go to a restaurant?'

'Look,' she began, 'please don't feel you have to entertain me just because we came out of the play early . . .'

Her voice trailed off uncertainly when she saw him frown. Unwilling to trigger off one of his unpredictable moods, she added quickly, 'The hotel would be nice.'

Wind knifed across the street as the commissionaire opened the swing doors for them.

'Cold enough for snow,' he grumbled as he let them out.

It was freezing. The few hundred yards to the hotel became a battle with the blistering wind. An empty milk carton hurtled down the street and there was not a soul in sight. By contrast the hotel was warm and welcoming.

He was surprisingly relaxed over dinner. Perhaps his laughter had relieved his irritability, or possibly the wine. He had been right about the hotel food. It was excellent, or perhaps it only seemed so because she was so hungry. Apart from the few chocolates in the theatre, she had eaten nothing since the picnic lunch in the car. She chose chicken and asparagus and he ordered a sparkling wine that was as pleasant to drink as champagne.

They talked about holidays and she told him about some of the old rectories she had had to cope with on *locum tenens* exchanges. Although she knew she was talking too much, she was aware that he found her amusing. He said little, but

48

his harsh expression had softened and he even laughed occasionally. She felt a growing sense of power, so much so that she believed that she could make him do anything. Not one to feel over self-confident with strangers, the experience was exhilarating.

'Your dress,' he said suddenly during a pause in the conversation. 'I meant to tell you – it is becoming.'

He spoke uncertainly like a man unused to paying compliments.

'Thank you,' she replied, looking at him over the rim of her glass and seeing not him, but herself reflected in the lens of his spectacles.

She looked away uneasily and saw herself again reflected in the huge mirror that lined the wall of the dining-room. For the second time that day she had difficulty in recognising the animated stranger in the tarty green dress. Once again the agonising pang of yearning contracted her womb and she was afraid. For too many years she had existed only as mother and wife on whom the lives of six people depended to such an extent that she had almost ceased to be a person in her own right. But now it seemed that the stranger in the mirror was taking over. There had been many times in the past when she had wanted to be a separate person with a separate identity, but now that it was within sight she was afraid of it. Up till now she had been bound by the shackles of family life. The stranger in the glass was a threat to these bonds, and perhaps not the only threat as she realised when she looked back at the man across the table.

With unreasonable urgency she wanted to escape. She wanted to ring Ken and hear his familiar voice reminding her of the telephone bill when she reversed the charge – Ken had always been a bit near over the telephone. With a sudden rush of home-sickness she wanted nothing else than to be the ordinary middle-aged parson's wife that she was. All day she had been playing a stupid game and to what end? she asked herself as she hurriedly drank her coffee. If she had won she had also lost, for she did not want the prize. It had been so long since she had played the sex game that she had forgotten how dangerous it could be. In future she would stick to the parsonage and spend her time knitting pullovers and writing to the boys. Clem had been right in one sense; she was too old for the games of youth.

They finished their coffee in silence and he did not try to detain her when she asked to be taken at once to Mary's house. Although he said little, concentrating on driving through the unfamiliar streets, she was aware of every movement he made, every breath he took, and she knew that he was aware of her.

'Tired?' he asked quietly, without turning his head.

'A little,' she replied, realising that she was exhausted. That morning with Ken seemed light years away.

'I shouldn't have dragged you up that hill,' he said, turning to her as they paused at some traffic lights. In the dark of the car she could not read his expression.

'It was fun,' she replied, keeping her tone light.

He said no more until they came to Mary's house. Then, switching off the engine, he said, 'The porter at the hotel said that snow was forecast for tomorrow. If the roads are still clear, I should like to start home a little earlier than we planned – say between three and four. That will give us an hour of the afternoon session.' He paused and added quietly, 'Under the circumstances I think it would be wise.'

'Whenever you like,' she told him.

He carried her overnight bag to the front door.

'Won't you come in and meet them?' she asked formally, and was relieved when with equal politeness, he refused.

She watched him walk down the path and suddenly remembered that she had not thanked him.

'George,' she called. It was the first time she had used his Christian name. He stopped and turned slowly.

'It was a nice evening. Thank you.'

He raised his hand in a brief unconfident gesture that brought back the pang of anguish with such flooding force that tears sprang to her eyes. Though the pain was the same, the cause was different. This time she was not yearning over her sons or her husband or even herself. This time she ached for him, for his insecurity, his loneliness and aloneness. For a moment she saw him as she imagined God might see him, vulnerable, lovable, and she trembled with compassion.

The moment of insight lasted less than a second. Shaking the tears from her eyes, she pressed Mary's bell.

6

Jim Cameron was one of the nicest men she knew. Certainly he was the most charming. In his presence she felt cherished and at ease. He was a lawyer with a practice in the city which had prospered not surprisingly, for his good-looking face and solicitous manner inspired a confidence that was not misplaced.

He met her at the door and after they had embraced affectionately he explained that Mary had gone to bed early as she was not well.

'Jim, I am sorry. You should have told me.'

'Nonsense. Mary would never have forgiven me if I'd said anything to put you off coming. We see far too little of you as it is. Besides, it gives me a chance to have you to myself for a change. When you and Mary get together I don't have a look in.'

Mary and she always had plenty to say to each other. They had been to school together and were the same age within months. It was through Mary that she had got to know Clem, and through Clem that Ken had got his present living. Although distance prevented their seeing much of each other, they had the sort of friendship that could be taken up where it had been left off the last time.

He took her into the living room and settled her in a corner of the large comfortable sofa in front of a huge log fire.

'Now tell me all about those boys of yours,' he said, handing her some whisky. 'How is the youngest enjoying his first term at school? You must miss him like hell.'

She was grateful to him for asking, and answered in detail, not afraid of boring him, for she knew he genuinely liked her sons. They adored him and not only because of the carefully thought-out Christmas presents or the birthday cheques that always arrived on the right day.

She gave him her youngest son's letter and knew that he would read every word before handing it back to her. There had been several events in the children's lives that had upset her until she had confided in him. She remembered how her two eldest boys had stolen a screwdriver, of all things, from Woolworths in full view of a member of the congregation, who had made a point of coming to tell her. There had been the time when her third son had been reported to the police for trespassing in a disused non-conformist chapel. After telling Jim about the incidents she had always felt better. He had that trick of shrinking trouble, of making rough edges smooth, partly because he was a good listener and partly because he never condemned. His advice was invariably comforting and its practical application usually sound. Only to speak of her family in this rich warm atmosphere was to enhance them in her heart. Uneasinesses settled, she leaned back more comfortably against the cushions and regarded her host with affection. She was grateful to him for making her life seem uncomplicated again. Even the Dean shrank to a proper place in the pattern of her life.

'Jim,' she said with a rush of warmth, 'you are such a comfortable person. Mary is so lucky.'

He stood up and took her glass over to the decanter.

'The other half?' he asked.

'But you are lucky too,' she continued, still in a state of

euphoria induced by the warmth and the whisky. 'Mary is so pretty and kind. She's made this house the most comfortable home I know. My old vicarage is like a barn in comparison. She must work hard to make everything so smooth-running and attractive, and yet she never seems ruffled or out of temper. I don't know how she does it.'

It was true; Mary seemed the perfect housewife living in an ideal home and yet managing to be nice with it. Alison had tried to achieve the same serenity in her own home. Her lack of success was only partly due to the fact that the drawing-room chimney belched black smoke in certain winds, and all the rooms needed a coat of paint.

'Perhaps Mary has no choice,' Jim replied reflectively.

'What do you mean? I don't understand.'

'I mean, my dear Ali, that things are seldom what they seem.'

'It isn't easy to simulate,' she said, looking at him curiously.

'It's the easiest thing in the world,' he told her seriously.

'You and Mary have the happiest marriage of any people I know.'

'Correction,' he said lightly. 'You and Ken probably have the happiest marriage of any two people I know.'

She was silent. She saw now that hers had been a stupid remark. What could she possibly know about their marriage except what they wanted her to know? It occurred to her that there were two distinct sorts of marriage, the one as intricate as the fusion of two personalities could make it, and the other simple, where the two personalities remained intact. Jim and Mary were in the former category, like lovers walking along the same road with arms entwined. She and Ken walked the same road side by side certainly, but apart.

And yet who was to say which was the happier marriage, the one that made demands or the one that allowed freedom?

Jim refilled his glass and came over to sit beside her on the sofa. He smelled of cigars and good soap, and for the first time in her life she was aware of his attractiveness. She took a mouthful of whisky and moved further into the corner of the sofa in an effort to discard the growing sensation of desire that had quickened her pulse. This was Jim, Mary's husband, a man she had liked as a brother for half her life. She frowned impatiently at herself.

'What is troubling you, Ali?' he asked presently. 'Is everything all right between you and Ken?'

She was immediately on the defensive. 'Of course. Why shouldn't it be? Why do you ask?'

'Because,' he said gently, 'for the first time in twenty years I think that you are aware of me as a man and not just as an unofficial uncle or an accessory of Mary. Am I right?'

She was ashamed and at the same time intrigued that he should have guessed her feelings so accurately.

'How do you know?'

'Because I have always been aware of you as a woman.'

Although his tone was light and she did not really think he meant it, she was amazed that the sexual awareness that had been growing slowly in her all day should have communicated itself to him. She wondered if the Dean had been conscious of it also, and a flicker of excitement passed over her.

'Have I shocked you?' he asked, amused.

She shook her head. 'What surprises me is that I can still shock myself.'

He laughed. Then he took her glass and set it down on the table behind them. He began to kiss her face very lightly, slowly and expertly. She did not move to encourage or restrain him, for she did not think that he was serious. Presently he moved his head back a little to look at her.

'Women are my weakness,' he said. His tone had changed and his eyes moved to her mouth. She knew then that he was no longer in a teasing mood.

'What about Mary?' she asked quietly, knowing that it was time to put an end to this madness.

He sighed and moved away from her.

'How little we know of each other. You and Ken, Mary and me. For twenty years we've exchanged letters and gifts, compliments and confidences, and yet what do you really know about me or Mary, if it comes to that?'

'I know the important things.'

'What important things? Do you know, for instance, that I've been unfaithful to Mary more times than I care to remember, and that she's left me twice?'

His words stunned her.

'But she's always come back?' she asked hesitantly.

'Yes, thank God, because I suppose she knows that although I sleep with different women from time to time, I prefer to live with her.'

'Then I do know the important things,' she said softly.

Knowing that all she had to do was to look at him, she wondered what it would be like to sleep with him. Delightful while it lasted; possibly delightful in retrospect. Jim was too tidy-minded to leave a trail of broken hearts. She thought of Mary upstairs, alone, and the little glow of lust that had flared so briefly, died. At the same time, she wondered how she would feel if Ken were to make love to Mary. The idea was so ludicrous that she could not imagine it, yet, she asked herself, why should it be so strange? Being a priest did not automatically exclude him from what he would call the sins of the flesh and Mary was beautiful. She had a sudden

56

image of them together, and was compelled to laugh out loud.

Jim looked at her with surprise, so she forced the faintly hysterical bubble of laughter to subside, and said:

'I was trying to imagine how I'd feel if Ken wanted to have sex with someone else.'

'You would mind,' he told her.

She thought of Mary's groomed appearance and excellent housewifery. She had not been particularly domesticated at school. She had had to work hard to keep her marriage. Alison wondered if she would work as hard to keep her own marriage if it were threatened. She had always taken it for granted. She and Ken made few demands on each other emotionally. There had never been time for introspection or philandering. A close relationship took years of patience and understanding. Up till now there had been no time, and now that there was time, she did not know if she would be prepared to work for it. She did not know if she even wanted it. It occurred to her that a marriage such as Jim and Mary's must be all the stronger for the knocks it had taken. Their marriage seemed like a fortress compared with which hers was a wide-open plain. She shivered suddenly as if the attack had already come, and stood up.

'I think I'll go to bed. Shall I see Mary in the morning?'

'Of course,' he said.

He took her hand and held it lightly for a moment. 'I apologise for acting the goat. I've had several worries recently . . .'

She would not let him continue.

'Next time, try biting your nails,' she said, and they both laughed.

The pink bedroom glowed with shaded lights; the painted biscuit box by the bed, the central heating, the private bathroom, the scalding scented water, all cherished and relaxed her exhaustion. She thought about Jim and came to the conclusion that he had not done anything so very wrong. Adultery and fornication were not words that one could connect seriously with Jim. Gracious living and charming manners cushioned the harsh realities. In her heart she did not think any the less of him for sleeping with his secretaries or clients, or whoever he chose to make love to. She was rather pleased that he had wanted to make love to her. As she lay back in the steaming bath she wondered what had happened to her old standards and morals. Over the years she had lost her ability to be shocked by anything, and she wondered if this were a good or a bad thing.

Just before she fell asleep she thought about the Dean. She had a mental image of him alone in a cheerless hotel room and the thought was like an exciting secret. She wrapped it up and put it to the back of her mind, but like a child, she could not help returning to the hiding place from time to time to have another look.

7

She slept badly, never entirely losing consciousness until just before dawn when she dreamed she was making love in a dark wood. After it was over she found herself lying alone on damp grass while a chill wind blew decaying leaves across her body. She woke filled with loneliness and longing for love. Turning on her side, she wanted Ken's warmth, yet not Ken, for it had not been Ken who had been her dream lover. Closing her eyes again, she wondered why she had been so sure it was not her husband, and began to think about her sex life with Ken.

Right from the start of their marriage they had avoided the use of, or even talk of, contraception. At eighteen she would not have known whom to ask or what to ask for. Thinking back, she could not now remember whether she even knew of the existence of such things. She doubted whether at that time Ken could have brought himself to ask for a contraceptive device over a counter, much less send away for the furtively sealed plain envelope, even if he had approved the principle, which to begin with she assumed he did not.

Nine months after the wedding her first son was born. A year later she gave birth to another boy. Her mother with anger – it was the only time Alison had ever heard venom in her voice – spoke of Ken's selfishness and forced her reluctant husband to 'speak to him', as she put it. Whether he ever summoned the necessary courage to do so Alison never knew; certainly Ken never mentioned it. In the end a friend of her mother's gave her the address of a specialist who, for the price of twenty-five guineas, fitted her with an internal device which her father had to pay for. Nine months later she gave birth to her third son.

There followed an unsatisfactory period when Ken, whose fastidiousness was revolted each time, did his best with an assortment of rubber goods, but the fourth child was determined to be born. As Clem vulgarly put it, one look at Ken in pyjamas was obviously enough. Ken bore meekly his mother-in-law's increasing dislike and accepted his family doctor's suggestions, but, after the fifth child, he took matters into his own hands. There was no more intercourse between them except within the limits of the prescribed 'safe period'. Artificial contraception had proved unsatisfactory. Natural contraception could do no worse. Ken felt the hand of God in it, and perhaps he had been right. Certainly there were no more pregnancies.

To begin with, it was very hard. There were nights when she had lain awake listening to his sleep-breathing and prickling with frustration. They risked full intercourse only on the day before and after her period. Though she started no new pregnancies she was less fit than she had been when bearing or feeding her babies. At the time she attributed her edgy headaches to coping with five demanding little boys, but, looking back, she realised that this was only partly the cause. If she could have enjoyed the nights, she could have coped better by day.

Her parents had been wonderful, taking the little boys in turns for holidays to give her some relief. When they both died within months of each other, she found that they had been paying vast sums into an educational policy so that the boys could be sent to her father's public school when they reached the age of thirteen.

After a few years, however, Alison became used to the limited ration of sex. They reached a certain skill in love-making that was all the more pleasant for its infrequency. Both had learned to give each other a maximum amount of pleasure. Each time was an occasion and though she could not admit even now that it was an ideal arrangement, to-gether they had made it work. And yet, as she lay in bed and re-thought her marriage, she realised that it was not strictly true to say that together they had made it work. There had been nothing in the arrangement so positive as that. Nothing had been said; nothing planned. It was an arrangement that both had come to take for granted over the years. Had Ken been as highly sexed as the begetting of five sons seemed to suggest, it would not have worked at all. As it happened, he was as abstemious in sex as he was with other physical pleasures, and Alison had never thought any the less of him for it.

This was one of the reasons why, when the pill became available, she did not suggest that she should take it. She had thought about it and had it been available in the earlier years of her marriage, she would have probably started tak-ing it after the birth of their third child. She was thankful now that she had not, for she could not imagine life without her two youngest boys.

She remembered a conversation she had had with Clem after they had both listened to a radio talk on birth control.

'I suppose Ken disapproves of the pill,' she had said when Alison admitted to not using it. 'Either that or you must want more children.'

There was some truth in what she had said for even now

61

after so many children, she would not really mind if she were to conceive again.

Beattie woke her with a pot of tea and a comfortable smile. She had been with Clem and Mary's parents until they died, and now, after a series of arguments between the sisters as to who should give her a home, she spent six months with each of them in turn.

'How are Mr Osmond and the boys?' she asked as she poured the fragrant tea into a patterned cup.

'They're fine, Beattie. How is Mary this morning?'

Beattie's face clouded. 'Much the same, but she'll be telling you all about it herself, I expect. She asked if you would care to breakfast in her room as she won't be getting up till later.'

'Of course. I'd like that. What sort of day is it?' she asked, yawning.

Beattie peered through the pink velvet curtains.

'Cold enough for snow.' She turned and came over to the bed. 'Mr Jim says you are going home today. You'd do better to stay here for a few days if you'll pardon me saying so. You could do with the rest and some of us here could do with the company.'

There was nothing to prevent her staying. Ken would not mind if she were to stay for the whole week. She was tempted to accept. To relax in this four-star luxury, to bask in the warmth of Jim and Mary's friendship, was tempting, as was the thought of no chores, no responsibilities and above all, no sad little empty attic rooms.

But she said, 'I wish I could, Beattie.'

Mary was lying back, pale and pretty, on a mountain of frilly pillows. The room was filled with the scent of flowers and clean skin on fresh linen. Mary herself was the only discordant note. She looked miserable.

'What's wrong, darling? Is it a chill or something?' Alison asked as she kissed her cheek.

'Not exactly.' Mary turned her head away. Her gleaming nails rasped on the eiderdown as she clenched her fists. 'I suppose I may as well tell you. I've got to go into hospital at the beginning of the week – a hysterectomy.'

Alison covered the silk-cool fingers with her hand.

'Mary! Jim never so much as hinted . . .'

'I know. I told him not to tell you.'

'But why? I don't understand. Surely you knew how concerned we would all be.'

Mary withdrew her hand restlessly. 'I don't really understand myself. It's just that I can't bear the thought of people knowing and talking about me.'

'There's nothing to be ashamed of.'

'I know, I know,' she said impatiently. 'Jim and the doctor and Beattie, bless her, keep on saying it, yet that's the feeling I have. In a way I'll be spoiled, handicapped, if you prefer. I don't expect you to understand. Why should you? It's not happening to you.'

But Alison did understand. If it were to happen to her – but she shied away from the thought. Why should there be a difference between losing a finger, say, and losing a womb? Most women would prefer to lose the womb, or, as someone once said, take away the nursery but leave the playground. But not Alison, and not, apparently Mary. As there was fright as well as horror in her friend's expression, she forced herself to be reassuring.

'Nothing could spoil you, darling.'

'A friend of mine had a breast removed and it was virtually the end of her marriage,' Mary continued wretchedly.

'But you aren't having a breast removed, you won't look any different.'

What did it matter how you looked? she thought. It was how you felt. Could you still feel? Could you still have those contracting pangs of compassion?

'I might grow a beard or get fat – don't laugh, Alison – it's to do with hormones.'

Could that be all she was afraid of?

'Darling, you won't look any different, you won't be different. No one is going to point at you in the street and say. "There goes a wombless woman." '

'Don't make me laugh. It's not funny, and anyhow, Jim will know.'

'What difference can that make?'

What difference if the world knew? It was the being without that mattered.

'Jim likes women to be perfect.'

'I think Jim just likes women to be women.'

'That's exactly what I mean.'

Alison tried a different angle. 'There's one compensation. You won't have to worry about getting pregnant.'

Mary's eyes filled with tears. 'And that's another thing. For the past ten years I've tried so hard to have another child. I've been a hopeless failure.'

'You have Elaine. How can you call her a failure?'

'It's easy for you to talk. You have five sons. Five sons!' she repeated. 'To my one daughter. I still hoped – after all, I'm not forty yet . . . Things might have been different if I'd given Jim a son.'

'I'm not so sure Jim wanted a son,' Alison said thoughtfully.

'How can you say that? Look how good he is with your boys. He would have been a marvellous father to sons.'

'I don't know,' Alison spoke with a conviction she really felt. 'If you were to ask Jim if he would prefer five sons to

64

one Elaine, he would think you mad. He's a man who likes the admiration of women. He's happy to have you and Elaine worship the ground he treads on. Subconsciously he would look on sons as rivals to your affection. Instead of being the charming kind person we all know, he would become a crotchety old bull elephant not fit to live with.'

'Really, Alison, what a thing to say,' Mary said with a gleam of laughter in her tears.

'You know it's true.'

It was true that a womb did not only exist for the conception of children, but Mary was comforted. By the time Beattie arrived with breakfast, she was asking about Clem.

'Will you tell her for me?'

'I'm sure she'd rather hear about it from you.'

'I daresay she would, but I don't think I can face Clem's curiosity at the moment. She's getting so sex-conscious these days. Have you noticed?'

Laughing, Alison had to agree, but she did not think Clem was any more sex-conscious than herself or Mary. She was only more outspoken. Was everyone so sex-minded? she wondered, as she spread butter on her toast. Was it something to do with the age, or only with their specific ages? Perhaps it had something to do with too much time to think. When the boys were at home she never gave it a thought, but for the last day or so, it had never been entirely out of her mind.

'Do you regret not having a daughter?' Mary asked more cheerfully as she drank her coffee.

Alison smiled at the coincidence of the question so similar to her own to the Dean on the previous day. Strangely enough, she had never minded. Before the births of her three younger sons, she had hoped for a girl. Her old aunts had become more tight-lipped and disappointed with every subsequent male appearance, but when the midwife had told her each time that it was another boy she had been pleased. Perhaps she would have been more pleased if it had been a girl. She had no means of knowing, but she did not tell Mary this.

'Of course,' she said lightly, 'but I was never pathological about it, and nor need you be.'

She went over and sat on the edge of the bed. 'Jim loves you and nothing will change that. After the operation is over you're going to be twice as fit as you are now. Everything is going to be all right, but you know that, don't you?'

Seemingly, she had convinced Mary, but she was left with a strange sense of desolation. Time for a woman was so short. To reduce it by a few years seemed to her to be cruel.

Beattie put her head round the door.

'There's a vicar called for you, Mrs Osmond,' she said, 'I've put him in the drawing-room.'

'A vicar? Heavens, it must be the Dean!' She glanced at her watch. 'I'll have to fly. He doesn't like to be kept waiting as I found to my cost last night,' she added in mock consternation.

'What happened?' Mary asked, sensing a story.

Alison told her briefly of her arrival in the hotel the previous night in a new dress and of her cold reception. She made it into an amusing story, exaggerating where necessary to make Mary laugh. But as she spoke she was aware of her own disloyalty. It reminded her of the time she had listened to a bumbling confession of affection from a junior when she had been a sixth-form goddess. Moved and flattered, she had been kind to the child, but it had not prevented her turning the affair into a good story for her friends in the privacy of the sixth-form room. She had felt the same shaming pang of disloyalty then as she did now and wondered why she should feel so for it did not seem to her that the cases were comparable.

The Dean was standing in Mary's flower-filled drawing-room. Against the rich comfortable background, he looked grey and shabby as if he had not slept much. There was no trace of relaxation or well-being in his features and his expression reminded her of how he had looked when she had joined him in the hotel on the previous evening. As she moved across the room, buttoning her coat, she had the feeling that she had known him all her life.

'It was nice of you to come,' she said warmly. 'Mary Cameron sends her apologies for not coming to meet you, but she's not too well.'

'I'm sorry to hear that,' he said formally and glanced at his watch.

'Now don't tell me I'm late again,' she said lightly. 'We had no arrangement to meet this morning.'

'Nevertheless,' he replied, ignoring her flippant tone, 'if we are to be in time, I suggest we go at once.'

'I'm quite ready,' she told him.

As she took her place beside him in the car, she was once again strongly aware of a feeling of familiarity, this time coupled with a sense of excitement, like a child contemplating Christmas.

Mary and Beattie had again tried to persuade her to stay on for a few more days, and though, at the time, she had not fully recognised the true reason for her refusal, she knew now exactly why she had been so determined. Her relationship with the man beside her, whether real or imagined, was too intriguing to abandon.

'Did you have a comfortable night?' she asked him presently.

'Not particularly,' he told her, and added, 'what about you? Did you sleep well?'

'I never do in a strange bed.'

'Nor do I,' he said and turned to look at her.

Immediately the memory of her dream came crowding back to her conscious mind and she recognised the faceless lover who had pleased her so in the night.

As he edged the car forward with the rest of the traffic, she blushed at the memory of her dream and her secret knowledge of its protagonist. She now knew why he had seemed so familiar to her. It was often this way with her dreams. If she dreamed of a warm relationship with a friend or stranger, she felt warm towards that person long after the dream had faded from her mind. She remembered a time at school when she had dreamed she was being kissed by a battle-axe of a French teacher. For days after she had felt attracted to that unlikely woman and had even written a love poem about her.

'With any luck,' he said, and his voice brought her back to reality with a start, 'you should get a good rest in your own bed tonight.'

'With any luck,' she repeated quietly, 'so should you.'

8

'You're mad,' said Mrs Gerber-Hythe as she and Alison came into the committee-room together, 'quite quite mad to attempt that journey tonight. Just look at the weather.'

The wind had dropped, but a cold dank atmosphere had settled like a pall on the city.

'Probably,' she agreed, unwilling to argue.

'At the risk of repeating myself, why don't you and George spend the night with me? You can always get a train to-morrow.'

She was spared the embarrassment of making further excuses by the arrival of Martin Sharpe. After a swift glance round the room to see who had already arrived, he noticed her and came forward, hands outstretched in fulsome greeting. She knew that Martin pitied her and Ken their remote country living and his hearty but somewhat false concern for their welfare amused her, for Ken considered himself fortunate in having escaped city life. Most of the time Martin's attitude amused her too, but not always.

'Well, Alison, and how's that husband of yours thriving in the wilderness? Ha, ha, ha!'

She found his laugh particularly irritating.

'Happily,' she replied lightly.

'Brenda's in town this morning. She suggested you might care to lunch with us.'

Over Martin's shoulder she could see that the Dean was

watching her. His expression was indefinable, but its intentness disturbed her. Forcing her attention back to Sharpe, she could think of no adequate excuse for refusing to lunch with him; besides, his company, however dull, afforded a measure of protection. Protection from what? she asked herself impatiently; surely not from the Dean? Light glinted on his glasses as he turned to speak to the Convener who had just come in, and she knew that she needed protection from her own wild thoughts.

The morning was given over to the discussion of ecumenism. Here Alison was able to show some interest. Perhaps, she thought, it had something to do with her present state of spiritual deadness, that she could not see how the barriers that separated the churches were in any way important. She knew that many of the lay members of Ken's congregation felt unhappy about the exclusive nature of their communion. She contributed, therefore, some remarks to the general discussion which won the approval of the laity present but drew no response from the clergy. This did not disturb her, however, for she was used to cool treatment from the fathers when the laity presumed on their province.

'You don't tell a dentist how to draw teeth,' Ken had grumbled on several occasions, 'so why do all laymen think they can run the church?'

To Alison, the only thing that mattered where Christianity was concerned was kindness. She could not see how in love's name, anyone, heathen or hot gospeller, could be excluded from the altar of love. Religion was to her a matter of feeling, or of not feeling, as in her present state. To Ken, and no doubt to the other clergy present, it was not only a fact but also their bread and butter.

It took just three minutes of Martin and Brenda's company for Alison to remember just how much she disliked them as a partnership. Without Brenda, Martin's pomposity was tolerable and similarly, without Martin, Brenda's acidity was bearable. Together they were as unpleasant a mixture as castor oil and orange juice.

They had a particularly nasty habit of belittling people and their motives in an innocent-seeming way. After an hour of their company, she had a bad taste in her mouth, as if the act of listening alone were enough to involve her in their opinions. They always seemed to be in agreement in their thinking and their combined effect was as depressing as an empty church.

Brenda was waiting for them in the foyer of a large restaurant in the main street. Dowdily dressed, with scuffed heels and a shabby bag, she seemed to Alison, who had not seen her for over a year, to be a little pathetic. Her lifeless hair needed attention and she wore too much cheap lipstick. Alison remembered her once saying before a woman's meeting as she plastered her lips with crimson paint, 'No one will ever be able to call me a typical parson's wife.'

No one had ever suggested it, but not for the reason Brenda feared.

'There you are,' she said in her high faintly petulant voice, managing at the same time a smile for Alison and a sharp glance at her husband. 'I was beginning to give you up,' she laughed joylessly. 'I hope there's something decent left on the menu. It's not often we eat out.'

The restaurant was crowded, but they managed to find a table for three in an alcove at the far end.

'I suppose this will have to do,' she said unenthusiastically. 'Tucked away in the corner, we'll probably have to wait hours to be served.'

She loosened her coat, and then, turning to Martin, made him give a blow-by-blow account of the morning's events.

'But didn't you say anything?' she asked at intervals.

If Martin told her that he had spoken she wanted to know exactly what he had said and then added her own criticism; if he had said nothing, she rebuked him with her dry laugh.

'Surely that was an opportunity wasted, dear.'

Alison remembered that since the early years, she had always been pitifully ambitious for her husband.

'Alison spoke up nobly,' Martin said, with a sly sideways glance.

'Oh?' Brenda was immediately on her guard.

'Somehow I don't think the clergy approved,' Alison said with a faint smile.

'Well done you! Some of those stuffed dog-collars need to be let out a notch or two,' Brenda said warmly.

Alison knew and despised herself for the bitchiness of the thought, that Brenda was pleased because she believed Alison had made a fool of herself.

'Well, now, tell us how old Ken is,' Martin said pompously. 'Pity you ever went to that backwater. Not much chance of catching a bishopric there. Ha, ha, ha!' Although he laughed, Alison knew he meant it.

'You should never have let him settle there,' Brenda added. 'When I first knew Ken he was such a live wire.'

'What makes you think he is any different now?'

Alison studied the menu, determined not to show that she was beginning to get annoyed. Stupid, stupid, she told herself, to allow herself to be upset by such trifles.

'Oh, Ken's not idle, couldn't be, we all know that,' Martin said hastily. 'All the same, that sort of country existence could have a debilitating effect on a chap. You only have to look at Bill Downes to see what I mean.'

'We met him in the High Street one day last month,' Brenda said eagerly. 'My dear, have you seen him lately?'

Alison saw him frequently for his parish was near Ken's.

'If ever I saw a man gone to seed, it's poor old Bill. Apart from his rude offhand manner, he was needing a hair-cut and he has got so fat. Martin couldn't get a civil word out of him,' Brenda continued, leaning her elbows on the table.

'His wife died less than a year ago . . .' Alison began.

'We know all about that, of course, but even so, as Martin is always telling the congregation, if one is a true Christian, one should regard the death of a loved one as a matter for rejoicing, if you see what I mean.'

The waitress took their orders, but Alison had no appetite.

'How did you come down?' Brenda asked when she had made sure the waitress understood the order.

'George Tindall brought her,' Martin chipped in.

'Really?' Brenda laughed. 'Poor you.'

Alison noticed that she always laughed before making a snide remark.

'We mustn't be too hard on poor old George,' Martin said quickly, with a sly glance at Alison.

'Hard on him?' Brenda raised her eyebrows. 'I'm not being hard on him. I was merely sympathising with Alison for having had to put up with him all the way from Coolwater Bay.'

'George isn't so bad, really,' Martin said nervously.

It occurred to Alison that he had not mentioned the Dean's rudeness to him the previous afternoon, and he was anxious that she should not do so.

When it appeared that Alison was not going to say anything, Martin became bolder.

'We ought to pity the poor man. I've had it on good authority that he's heading for a breakdown.'

'Oh really?' Brenda leaned forward. 'Who told you that?'

Martin mentioned the diminutive Canon.

'He should know,' Brenda said with a laugh. 'I, for one, am not at all surprised. It's his wife I'm sorry for. We're both so fond of dear Joan. Do you know her well?' she asked Alison.

Alison shook her head. She was beginning to get angry. Determined to detach herself from the conversation, she thought of the last time she had made a conscious effort to be detached. Her eldest son had come from his first term at university with long straggling hair, a moustache and sideburns. She had thought it hard to say nothing then, but it had been child's play to the self-control she needed now.

How could Ken see anything in this odious, sick little man and his sicker wife? she asked herself. But Ken had a knack of getting the best out of horrors like Martin. His method was to talk about things rather than people. She remembered listening in an agony of boredom while he and Martin discussed endlessly the comparative merits of their respective cars. Now she knew why; wily old Ken.

'And how are you, Alison?' Brenda asked with her dry laugh as the waitress put plates of steak pie in front of them. 'You're looking tired, but that's hardly surprising I suppose. I often say to Martin that I don't know how you cope, don't I, dear?'

Martin nodded, his mouth full.

'Of course,' she continued, 'you're one of the lucky ones, aren't you?'

Alison raised her eyebrows.

'You don't have to scrimp and scrape on the minimum stipend like we do. Five sons all at public school is rather a give-away, isn't it?' She did not wait for a reply. 'Not that

I grudge it to you. Please don't think that. You need something to make up for all the drudgery, I suppose. But do you really think that public schools are all that worthwhile? Some of the boys I've met lately are – to put it kindly – not the shining examples of leadership they're supposed to be. In fact I would go so far as to say they were conceited layabouts without any common principles of decency.'

Alison was not going to get into an argument over the pros and cons of a public school education, particularly with Brenda, so she said nothing.

'I'm sure Alison's sons are not like that,' Martin began hastily. 'They're all fine boys, fine boys!' he repeated heartily.

'I was talking in general,' Brenda said coldly. 'We all know that Alison's children are perfect. Yes indeed, you are one of the lucky ones, did you but know it.'

A note of undisguised bitterness crept into Brenda's voice. Anxious to change the subject, Alison forced herself to ask pleasantly after the Sharpes' only daughter.

'How is Margaret?'

For a moment neither of them said anything and Alison was aware of their uneasiness. At last Martin spoke.

'Margaret? She's fine, just fine.'

Brenda put down her knife and fork with a clatter and pushed away her plate. 'How can you be so stupid, Martin? Alison knows well enough how Margaret is. What's the point in lying?'

'Is something wrong?' Alison turned from Brenda to Martin.

'I thought the whole diocese knew,' Brenda said bitterly.

'Knew what?'

'Margaret has been rather a silly girl,' Martin interposed, glancing pleadingly at his wife.

'Silly!' Brenda sneered.

Martin glanced uneasily at the next table, and Brenda, automatically susceptible to the opinion of others, lowered her voice. 'If that's what you call living in sin, she has indeed been silly.'

'I don't understand.' Alison, sensing tragedy, spoke softly.

'No, of course you don't. You've never had a daughter.'

'Brenda, please,' Martin said desperately. 'You know we agreed not to . . .'

'Leave me alone,' Brenda said sharply. 'Alison asked a question which I've a mind to answer. Alison and her precious sons! Did you know it was a boy like one of your toffee-nosed public-school sons who did this to Margaret? She was good enough to fornicate with, but not good enough to marry.'

'Brenda!' Martin was genuinely shocked. Fornication was a word he hesitated to use even in church.

'Is Margaret . . ?' Alison began.

'She's expecting a child,' Martin said miserably.

'She's pregnant,' Brenda said simultaneously. 'Pregnant without a husband, without a home and without a farthing so far as we know.'

Remembering Margaret, Alison had a mental image of a thin dark girl with greasy hair and little to say for herself. Throughout an afternoon visit some years back, she had contributed one remark to the conversation. Brenda had been boasting with maternal pride on the amount her daughter did to help in the parish, especially with the Sunday School. While the others had talked generally, Ken had turned to her and asked her how she enjoyed teaching the children. She had looked up from one of the boys' comic books and dared him to be shocked.

'It's a bloody waste of time,' she had said.

Ken had been sufficiently moved and sorry for the girl to report the conversation to Alison later. They had both been glad when they heard that Margaret had achieved university and hoped she might find happiness away from the demands of the parish and her parents. Seemingly she had not.

'Poor Margaret,' Alison said with compassion.

'Poor Margaret, indeed!' Brenda flashed. 'Is that all you can say? And what about us, may I ask? After all we've done, all she's been taught. Apart from the shame and degradation she's brought on herself, what about us?'

'But she didn't mean . . .'

'I'm not so sure. Sometimes I wonder. We have always tried to set an example to the parish. People expect clergy families to be blameless in certain respects. And then Margaret comes home, flaunting her sin, proud of it, expecting us to condone it. I sometimes think she did it on purpose just to shame us. She's always despised us for trying to lead decent Christian lives. This has been her revenge. But we showed her we were not going to lower ourselves to her standards. I told her quite bluntly that as she sowed so must she reap. The vicarage was not a home for unmarried mothers or a refugee camp for illegitimate children.'

'You – what?' Alison could not believe that she had heard right.

Brenda looked at her suspiciously.

'We asked her to make her own arrangements. Is that so surprising?'

'You turned her out?'

'I wouldn't put it quite like that,' Martin began.

'You turned her out!'

Alison stood up, feeling heat sweep over her in waves.

She crossed the restaurant and began to buy buns indiscriminately at the bakery counter. The bloody prigs, she thought, the abominable bloody prigs. She would have liked to walk out of the restaurant, but, as she paid for her purchases, she realised she had left her coat at the table.

Martin was alone, paying the bill.

'Brenda's gone to the Ladies,' he said uneasily. 'She's upset; you understand.'

'Martin,' she said, keeping her voice calm, 'I'd like Margaret's address.'

'Margaret's address?' He looked at her stupidly.

'I'd like to offer Margaret a home.' She didn't know she was going to say it till it had been said.

He folded his wallet and put it back in his pocket before speaking.

'I don't think Brenda would like that.'

'The hell with what Brenda likes,' she said, allowing her anger to show. 'I'm thinking of Margaret.'

'I can't help you then,' he said coldly, rising to help her put on her coat. Then he added in a conciliatory tone, 'I don't know where she is.'

'You don't know?' She sat down again, disregarding the frustrated glance of the waitress who was hoping to clear the table. 'Look, Martin, I know it's none of my business what you and Brenda do but . . .'

'You're right,' he said, 'but as you seem to have made it your business, I'll tell you the facts. Margaret came to us as Brenda told you, when she knew she was pregnant, but she did not ask us to give her a home or advice or even money. She came, as Brenda said, to flaunt herself. She acted as if she was pleased with herself and part of her pleasure came from watching our reaction. She said some unforgettable things. Brenda was broken-hearted. Is that so strange to you? We both said things we didn't mean, but she goaded us into saying them. If she had come to us wanting help, do you think we would have refused her? She's our only child.'

It sounded reasonable. She could imagine Margaret's sense of inferiority and shame driving her into a dreadful false pride.

'But surely,' she argued, 'you could have offered her a home.'

'Now, Alison, where is your sense of proportion? How could I have stood in the pulpit Sunday by Sunday and preached about sin with my own daughter sitting in the vicarage pew, swollen with adultery?'

'You could try preaching about love,' she said, and, picking up her gloves, prepared to go. 'Goodbye, Martin.'

He rose quickly. 'Wait a moment, won't you? Brenda will be back soon.'

'Thanks for the lunch,' she said, and left him.

She passed Brenda coming out of the cloakroom. She had been crying. Drawing her aside to a couch in the foyer, she said, because she could not stop herself:

'Brenda, please try to find Margaret and offer her a home. Be kind to her for your own sake as much as for hers. I think you make too much of what she's done. She's a young girl and she fell in love. What's so wrong with that? You make it add to so much more.'

Brenda's mouth, under a fresh application of lipstick, tightened. There was no trace of tears now.

'It's as I always suspected. You are one of those modern thinkers who seem to think that chastity and morality don't matter any more. Let me tell you, they matter to us. Why should we condone adultery just because our daughter commits it?'

79

For the first time in years, Alison wanted to say something about Christ, but she could not do it. She could not bring the sad-eyed God of her imagination into this sordid little affair. The one had no relevance to the other as far as she could see. Let Martin and Brenda go back to their snug little world of church services and vicarage teas. How safe they were, surrounded by their dwindling congregation, cut off from the world. God's house, they called it, but they had made it God's tomb. Margaret was well out of it.

9

Alison hurried back to the committee-room. Breathing the icy air deeply, she welcomed its sting and lash on her face. Her longing to escape was more than merely a need to get away from the Sharpes. The whole church whose representatives they all were, with its restricting views and narrow moralities, seemed to her to be stifling. She had a need to reassure herself that its closed world still contained fair-minded people with kindly principles.

She was early and the only person already arrived whom she knew was the Dean. He was standing by the window talking to one of the younger clergy, a man she knew only by sight. She went over to join them. They stopped talking and turned with some surprise to look at her wind-stung cheeks and crusading eyes. Although she could think of nothing to say, no reason to give for interrupting their conversation, she was not embarrassed. The Dean introduced her to the younger man, and they stood talking about nothing in particular for a few moments. Out of the corner of her eye she saw Martin come into the room and give her a quick reproachful glance.

'I'm ready to leave whenever you like,' she told the Dean, deliberately avoiding Martin's eyes.

'It all depends on when the boundary report is to be made. I have to make a statement.' The Dean studied his watch. 'It's high time we started,' he added impatiently.

A moment later the Convener asked the members to take their places. She passed Martin on her way to the end of the table. His small mouth was pouted in concentration as he inclined his head deferentially towards a retired colonel with a double-barrelled name. The colonel was clearly not impressed with Martin, not from any attitude of rank or breeding, but because Martin, in spite of his pompous manner, spoke as a man without authority. With a flash of malice, she visualised him reporting back to Brenda how he had had such an interesting discussion with the dear colonel. But as always, her malice was short-lived. As she watched him, Martin raised his hand to emphasise a remark and she caught a glimpse of his rough red hands. She remembered how hard he worked in the thankless nettle-rank vicarage garden; how he humped coals to Brenda's upstairs sitting-room in the house that was so close to the railway that it was never free of grime. Suddenly Alison was shaken with pity for them both. It occurred to her that the burden of Margaret's behaviour was too heavy for their puny shoulders. Someone in the Bible had once said that no one was tired beyond their ability to cope. If that were the case, Martin and Brenda had had a raw deal.

The afternoon wore slowly on. The Dean spoke eventually and at length. He was obviously as good a committee man as she had been led to believe. After the hideous lunch party, she found that her feeling of affection towards him had increased in proportion to her feelings of contempt for the Sharpes. The Sharpes were also responsible for another change in her outlook. Whereas before she had been partly ashamed, afraid even, of her interest in the Dean, now she did not care. It was as if she were saying, 'I like him, so what? I dreamed about him, so what?' Prudish disapproval was not going to be part of her make-up.

It was almost four when the Dean caught her eye and they both excused themselves from the meeting. Mrs Gerber-Hythe came out with them in order to give Alison a bag complete with thermos and sandwiches which she had made up during the lunch break.

'I still think you're mad,' she said as she handed her the parcel, 'but no one ever pays any attention to me, least of all the clergy.'

Alison kissed her expensive powdery cheek and received in return an equally warm embrace. She looked up to see the Dean watching her with the same still intentness that she had noticed before and involuntarily she shivered.

'I'm coming,' she told him, and ten minutes later they were driving through the suburbs.

Because it was on her mind and because she was convinced that he would think as she did on important matters, she began to speak about the Sharpes.

'I lunched with Martin and Brenda Sharpe today.' She paused, and when it became obvious that he was not going to answer, continued, 'I'd like to tell you about it if I may. I need to get the whole thing into perspective.'

'If you are assuming that because I spoke sharply to Sharpe yesterday, I am interested in gossip about his family, you are mistaken,' he said coldly.

For a moment she was surprised into silence. She had felt so close to him that she had assumed that he would feel the same way about her. Now she saw that there was no reason why he should do so. It was not he who had had the dream. She was, however, not so easily put off.

'Is it such a sin when an unmarried girl gets pregnant by the man she loves?' she asked.

'You are still talking about Martin Sharpe,' he replied coldly.

83

'Well – hardly,' she said with a faint smile.

He was not amused. 'You don't really expect me to say that co-habiting before marriage is a good thing.'

'No, I suppose not. It just seems to me to be so much less of a sin than unkindness and blind stupidity,' she replied, thinking of Brenda's attitude to her daughter.

'Who is to judge which is the greater sin, physical lust or lust in the heart; physical violence or mental cruelty? The New Testament makes no distinction.' His voice had dropped so that he seemed to be talking to himself rather than to her.

'If you had a child . . .' she began, thinking of Margaret.

'But you forget, I have no child,' he lashed out savagely. 'Why trouble me with your hypotheses? You can answer the question five times over yourself.'

He was shaking and his knuckles stood out white against the steering wheel. She was appalled. Compared with the Sharpes he had seemed to her to be a rock of justice and commonsense. She had not expected such a reaction to what, after all, had been a harmless question. Remembering what Martin had said regarding his mental health, she began to wonder whether there might be some truth in it. She knew she ought to leave well alone, to change the dangerous course of the conversation, yet she could not do it. She was excited in a strange almost nauseated way.

'Do you perhaps,' she began carefully, knowing that she was risking more of his anger and yet unable to stop herself. 'Do you perhaps resent me for having children?'

He took his eyes off the road for a moment and looked at her. It was the same intent look as she had noticed before, again so swift that she could not interpret its message. Then he said in a different tone that was almost pleading:

'How could I?'

84

She was swept by a surge of sexual desire so hot that it suffused her whole body with blood. She knew that this time the dream was not responsible for the sudden sweat of lust. This time, her desire was real and wholly associated with the man beside her rather than with the faceless fantasy lover of her dream.

And what a pretty feeling it was. She closed her eyes the better to enjoy the throb in her groin, the sweet beat deep in her womb. It had been a long time since she had last felt the sweeping waves of lust. She had almost forgotten how intoxicating it could be. As she lay back in the car seat, she found herself remembering the first time.

She had been seventeen at the time and in her first term at university. She had never been out with a man before and she had gone to a students' hop in the hopes of making a boyfriend. She had stood on her own for what seemed like hours among the noisy beer-swilling undergraduates and felt wretched. Her mean ration of self-confidence had almost run out and she was on the point of going home when a fat boy with round glasses and a king-sized cigarette asked her to dance. She nodded although aware that this chubby catch was possibly more shaming than an empty net.

Surprisingly he danced well and she accepted an invitation to go out with him the following week. As the days passed and they saw more of each other she found him nicer than his looks suggested.

'What on earth do you see in him?' her friends asked, and she found it a difficult question to answer.

'He makes me laugh,' she replied and it was true enough, though not for the reasons her friends assumed. He was a genuinely witty man, totally different from any other person of her limited acquaintance; also he was male.

As long as it was dark and she did not have to look too

closely at his chubby bespectacled face she was happy to have him kiss her. He smelled of soap and his skin was almost as soft as her own. She grew to enjoy the feel of his hand in hers and the long motionless kisses in the back row of the cinema.

One evening he told her his landlady was away and when he invited her to his rooms for supper, she accepted. He produced a splendid meal, far better than she could have prepared, and after they had washed up he put out the light and settled beside her on the couch. They kissed for a long time and then his hand settled hot and trembling on her knee. After what seemed like an age his hand began to move with agonising slowness to her thigh above her stocking. Her whole consciousness was concentrated on that moving hand. She wanted it to reach her softest part, but it never did.

Within a few days she had met a more prepossessing youth. The fat boy sent her a few desperate letters, one containing a proposal of marriage, but by now he was no longer interesting. Years after, she realised that he had been as shy and ignorant of her flesh as she had been of his. After him there had been others, each of whom had taken her a step further in the game of sex, but every time the fire of lust burned in her womb she remembered the fat boy for he had been the first to light that hot sweet flame.

IO

When she opened her eyes, it was snowing. Fine white dust swept across the dry road, danced in the headlights and ticked on the windscreen. A sudden heavier flurry hurled itself on the glass and the Dean switched on the wipers. Alison was not surprised to see the snow. The threat of it had always been there and she had known it would come, just as, she suspected, he had known it too. She watched, hypnotised by the swirling gyrating gold-tinged abandonment of the flakes. The verges sparkled in the lights and the fields beyond had become white lakes.

The snow made her think of the boys, three of them on the big sledge bumping and screaming their way down the hill behind the village, and herself stomach down on the toboggan with the two babies on her back, incapable of steering, hurtling into a convenient drift. She dismissed the carefree memories impatiently. The present situation was too intense to allow intrusions from the past.

The Dean slowed to a crawl for it had begun to blow a blizzard outside.

'Aren't you going to say "I told you so?" ' he asked.

She started. It had been so long since either of them had spoken that his voice sounded obtrusive in the warm cocoon of the ear.

'I expect Mrs Gerber-Hythe is thinking it,' she said.

'It may only be a local shower.' He paused and added in a different tone, 'Aren't you worried?'

'Worried?' she repeated. The question surprised her. 'Should I be?'

'Women usually get in a panic about having an accident or getting delayed, don't they?'

She could not imagine herself panicking with the Dean in command, yet had she been caught in a similar situation with her older sons or even with Ken, she would have been gripping her seat secretly and tensing at every corner. But what was the use of panic now? she asked herself. There was an inevitability about the whole journey that made a mockery of conventional attitudes.

Presently the snow eased a little, but gusts of icy wind sent the loose flakes scudding across the road and found every crack in the car. Even with the heater, she began for the first time to feel cold. There was a tartan rug on the back seat and when she had tucked it round herself she felt a little warmer. After a few more miles it began inevitably to snow again. This time there was nothing fitful or gusty in the fall. It was snowing in earnest. The wipers cleared fans on the caked screen, but the side and rear windows soon became opaque white walls. Still they edged on, inch by careful inch. The first time they got stuck, in a drift that had formed across the centre of the road, he got out to dig the car clear.

He's mad, she thought; he must be mad to consider going on. But if he were mad, then so was she, for she had said not one word to dissuade him. Their wisest course would be to stop at a hotel. Her imagination, racing ahead, placed them together in a warm carpet-hushed vestibule. She could see the sleepy incurious receptionist, the tidy conventional bedrooms and the turned-down waiting beds. The gulf that existed between her imagination and the real situation seemed to narrow a little. The game was getting out of hand.

88

Veering from the wild train of her thoughts, she looked round for something to distract her attention, to remind her that she was a woman of nearly forty with five sons and not an irresponsible girl. Her eye fell on Mrs Gerber-Hythe's thermos and sandwiches and she began to unpack them.

His coat and bare head were soaked with melting snow when he got back into the car. She handed him a mug of coffee. It was scalding, and his hands, red and raw with cold, hugged it gratefully, but he refused to eat. She watched the last of the snow-flakes turn to water on his coat before she spoke.

'We won't make it, will we?' she said, leaning over to refill his cup.

'I don't know.'

He drank too quickly, spilling some on his coat. She watched the dribble of coffee trickle down his black burberry and mingle with the melted snow.

'Perhaps it would be wise to stop off at the next hotel,' he said, not looking at her.

'Yes,' she agreed quietly.

A pulse began to beat in the pit of her stomach. He engaged gear and drove on towards the mountains. It occurred to her that it would have been more sensible to turn back for they had just passed through a town bristling with boarding houses, and as far as she could remember it was some distance to the next hotel. But she said nothing.

After a mile or so the car stuck again. The engine roared as the wheels skidded helplessly in the mass of snow. She opened her window and saw that they were only several yards from a lay-by. She pointed it out to him and offered to take the wheel while he cleared a path.

'At least we won't be a danger to anyone else on the road.'

He agreed, and after half an hour's labour, the car was safely wedged against a litter-bin which had been entirely covered with snow until she hit it.

When he got back into the car shivering and wet through, she slid back into the passenger seat.

'I've done my best,' he said, more to convince himself than to her. 'I can do no more.'

Both of them knew it had not been enough.

He switched off the headlights but kept the sidelights on. The only light in the car came from the illuminated dashboard. The clear fans on the windscreen soon caked over with snow and they were alone. The whole world shrank to the space inside the car. He peered at the petrol gauge which registered less than a quarter full and then he switched off the engine. The only sound was the heavy roar of the snow-filled wind.

'What are we going to do?' he asked in a low voice.

She supposed she should feel a sensible sort of anxiety on Ken's behalf if not her own, and indeed she was aware of the sickening uneasiness that sometimes anticipates disaster. It was a sensation strange to her and one with which she did not know how to cope properly. She glanced at him. His hair glistened with water in the dim light. He was still gripping the wheel and he had begun to shiver in earnest. He was thoroughly chilled. Remembering how ill he had seemed to be on several occasions the previous day, she was worried.

She had always been good with illness. There was nothing she enjoyed more than fussing over the boys when they were ill. She often thought that if she had to choose a career for herself now, she would be a nurse. It gave her great satisfaction to be able to give comfort. Touching a pulse, smoothing a brow were legitimate services available to stranger and relation alike. All her previous thoughts and desires could be channelled into deeds of practical humanity.

'First of all,' she said, trying to sound brisk and efficient, 'you are going to take off that wet coat before you catch a chill and then we're both going to get into the back of the car and try to get some rest.'

She might have been talking to one of her children who had come in with wet feet. The only difference was that he did not attempt to argue.

He left her to adjust the back seats so that they could both lie down in comparative comfort, but once outside the car he hesitated, standing by the open door.

'What is it? What's wrong?' she called.

He did not answer immediately, and then he leaned down and put his head in the door.

'I can see a light over there about fifty yards from the road. It looks like a house.'

'Are you sure?' she asked. 'I don't remember seeing any houses on this particular stretch of the road.'

'There are several – forestry houses, I believe. I'll go and see if anyone can offer us shelter.'

There was a hesitancy in his tone that was uncharacteristic, almost as if he were hoping she would try to dissuade him.

'It seems only sensible,' he added, still not moving.

A flurry of fresh snow burst into the car which was now Arctic cold. She could see that he was still shivering.

'Of course,' she agreed quickly. 'You're right. I'll come with you.'

She reached behind for her overnight bag.

The wind seized the door from her hand and would have broken the hinge if he had not been there to catch it. Her long suède boots sank up to her knees in soft snow, but he did not attempt to help her. Instead he took her bag and shone his torch on the top of the five-barred gate that led to the cottage whose light was now clearly visible, shafting palely through the storm.

She followed in his wake, matching her steps to his, while the wind threw fistfuls of frozen snow into her face. At the gate she turned to look back at the car, but there was no time for regret. He was waiting for her to climb over the gate. He did not offer to help her until her foot slipped on the icy wooden spar. He caught her by the hand and the contact quickened her whole body so that she could not let go. Nor did he attempt to draw away, but gave her the torch to hold while he picked up their two bags in his other hand. The cold of his flesh penetrated the wool of her glove so that in the moment of contact she understood the point where fire and ice become indistinguishable.

She was still holding his hand when they reached the cottage. It was the first thing that Mrs Beck noticed.

'Standing there like a couple of lost lambs, hand in hand,' she told her shepherd husband later when she rejoined him in the big brass bed. 'You could have knocked me down with a feather when I saw it was a parson and his missis.'

It was a natural mistake to make. Less natural was the fact that neither Alison nor the Dean made any attempt to correct it.

Mrs Beck was a forceful personality. She was enormously fat because she could never resist her own cooking. She was quick-witted, garrulous and hospitable, the sort of woman not easily discounted and yet afterwards Alison could remember little about her except her name, and even of that she was never quite sure.

The cottage kitchen shone with brass, black lead and silver cups, Institute trophies for decades of inspired baking. Texts adorned the walls and a great black mat of a collie dog occupied most of the available floor-space, yet all Alison was to remember afterwards was the sickening smell of over-blown hyacinths from a bowl on the table which was to assault her memory from time to time for the rest of her life.

'Come in, come in, the pair of you.'

Mrs Beck overwhelmed them with her warmth while the sleepy dog thumped an unenthusiastic tail.

'I was just saying to him in his bed in the room that there'll likely be someone stranded on the road tonight. It's as wild a night as I can remember and I've known some pretty rough ones on the moors hereabouts. Eh, but you are wet! Give me your coats and I'll hang them in the scullery for now.'

Alison did not look at the Dean as they took off their coats and handed them to Mrs Beck, but she was aware of every move he made. So conscious of him was she that the dominant presence of the stout shepherd's wife had a dream-like quality about it.

'Eh, I am glad I left a good fire on. I just said to him in the room that I'd best be prepared. You'll take a bite of supper and some'at hot?'

He had stopped shivering, but his hands as he held them towards the fire shook a little.

'It's very good of you,' he murmured. 'We would be most grateful if we could perhaps spend the night by your fire, or at least until the snow eases a little.'

'You'll do no such thing,' she interrupted indignantly. 'You will sleep in a proper bed like civilised folk and you'll not refuse a bowl of hot soup. You looked starved with cold and hunger, the pair of you.'

'We don't want to be a bother,' Alison said, her voice sounding unnatural in her own ears.

'Bother!' Mrs Beck cried, pouring soup from a basin into a pan and putting it on the stove to heat. 'We're put on God's earth to bother, aren't we? You, a parson's wife, should know that, I should think. I keep the upstairs room ready for travellers like yourselves. You won't need me to tell you what it says in the good book about entertaining strangers, now will you? All I have to do is put a bottle in the bed and a light to the heater.'

Soon the table was spread with the makings of a feast. Pastries, home-made bread, fruit-cake surrounded the bowls of thick potato soup that steamed up at her. She dipped her spoon into the thick broth and at the same time raised her eyes. He was watching her. Slowly she returned the spoon to her plate. Her hunger was not for food. I want him, a small interior voice said so distinctly that for a moment she thought he must have heard.

It seemed hours before they could politely escape the suffocating hospitality of their hostess, but at last she led the way up the narrow cottage stair which creaked and shook alarmingly under her weight.

For a moment Alison thought he was not going to follow and disappointment made her faintly giddy. Her ears strained for the sound of his step on the stair, but she could hear nothing but the roar of the wind and the chatter of her hostess as she slipped a stone hot water bottle wrapped in soft flannel into the bed and folded the candlewick cover.

'Well, I'll leave you now. You'll be dead tired, I'm thinking. If there's anything you want, you just have to ask, mind. We don't stand on ceremony here.'

'Yes – thank you,' Alison said, moving with her to the

94

door, willing her to be gone, not caring if she sounded un-gracious or impatient.

The room was so small that the bed occupied most of the available space. An ancient black paraffin heater made intricate lacy patterns on the ceiling and filled the room with a warm glow when she turned off the light. A flurry of snow beat on the curtained window as she quickly took off her clothes and put on her bath-robe, tying it loosely at the waist. When eventually she heard his foot on the stair her heart was beating so strongly that it was not until he opened the door, stooping under the low lintel, that she was sure it was really him.

They stood looking at each other across the small room. Her body was full of pleasurable sensations that she had not felt for years.

'I'll give her ten minutes or so to clear up downstairs and then I'll leave you in peace,' he said quietly.

'Come and get warm,' she said, holding out her hand, but he did not move.

'You're still so wet,' she said, moving towards him and touching the sleeve of his jacket. 'You ought to get out of these things before you catch pneumonia.'

Her voice sounded strange in her own ears, soft, greedy, eager. Slowly she ran her hand down his arm. It gave her intense pleasure to touch him. She felt his body tense at her touch and her own fired in quick response. She lifted his hand in both of hers.

'How cold you are,' she said, drawing him closer to the stove.

And once again she could not let go. It was as if his body had become a magnet to her flesh. Every cell was drawn towards him. A hot blush crept upwards from her breast to her face. She lifted his hand and carried it to her flaming cheek. At the same time he gripped hers and carried it to his lips.

'Alison,' was all he said, but she knew that he wanted her at least as much as she wanted him. She was enchanted with the power of her sex. The measure of his desire must, she believed, match the extent of her desirability and the knowledge of this was sufficient to bring her lust to a new peak. And yet, although the physical changes that were taking place in her worked hard to blind her to sensible considerations, amazingly she hesitated. It was not that she cared a pin for the moral implications. Fornication and adultery were words that formed part of the Sharpes' vocabulary, not hers. She was just within the safe period of her menstrual cycle. Generous by nature, she believed that it would be easy for her to give pleasure to this man, who, she felt, had had little enough of it in his life. Besides, Mrs Gerber-Hythe had asked her to be kind to him. In this way her mind worked, making excuses, paving the way for what she wanted to do, and yet there was still a niggle of anxiety which made her pause.

Just before she made up her mind – and it was up to her, she knew that – she had a vision of the night that lay ahead if she were to withdraw now. She knew she was not strong enough to put out the furnace she had lit in her own body, let alone his. Gently she withdrew her hand and, reaching up, took off his glasses.

'We're playing with fire,' he said, not moving.

'It's a good way to keep warm,' she whispered, aware of an idiotic surge of excitement as she reached back to put his glasses on the chest of drawers. Curving her hand round his neck, she drew his face down to hers. For a second it seemed that he was going to resist, but when her mouth touched his, he shuddered and in a moment his arms were round her and he was kissing her face, her neck and her eyes.

'I love you,' he told her again and again. 'Jesus, Mary, but I love you.'

Troubled by the blasphemous quality of his feelings, she stiffened. She had not thought of love. Love was a burden she was not prepared to carry. Sex was all she wanted and all she was prepared to give. There were too many commitments already on her heart.

He sensed her withdrawal.

'I'm sorry,' he said, lifting his head immediately, 'I've no right . . . forgive me.'

But she could not let him go.

'Be calm,' she said, caressing the back of his neck with one hand and tracing his mouth with her forefinger. 'Be calm,' she said again, and put her lips where her finger had been. Her mouth opened and her tongue moved forward to touch his. He groaned and the sound melted her. Her secret places slackened and warmed. Her breast ached. They stayed pressed together, fused from thigh to lips until presently she drew away from him. She loosened the sash of her robe, and let it fall from her shoulders. Taking his hands she guided them to her breasts. As his cold fingers touched her flesh he seemed to stop breathing. For a moment she thought she had gone too far and that she would be left as the fat boy had left her in a state of suspended lust. She was no schoolgirl to call a halt after the first feel. Up till this moment she had not consciously thought how far they would go together. Now she knew. The game begun would be finished.

Her anxiety proved unnecessary. With shaking exploratory fingers he touched her breasts. She could feel wonder in his hands as he traced their softness. He bent to kiss them, moving his mouth towards the nipple, touching it with his tongue; and then he sucked. Her body arched as the familiar agony contracted her womb. This yearning anguish could only be relieved in one way. She had to have him in the core of her. She lifted his head from her breast and brought his mouth to her lips; then she reached down and felt for his groin.

'I love you,' he said. 'Oh God, how I love you. I have always loved you from the beginning of time.'

This time the words did not disturb her. For the moment she loved him too.

'Come to bed,' she whispered, her fingers busy with the stud that fastened his clerical collar.

And now for the first time he took the initiative in their love-making. It was a strange intercourse, clumsy, rough like the fumblings of unskilled youth and altogether too quick and impatient. His mounting excitement awoke in her the beginnings of a response, but his climax came too soon and he did not tell her when he was ready, as Ken had learned to do, so that her own climax was diminished and disappointing. Presently she shifted, aware of his weight and wanting him to move, but he only held her closer.

'Not yet,' he said.

She felt a warm wetness on her neck and with a sense of shock realised it was tears. His grief or shame, she could not tell which, was even harder to bear than his physical weight, so that she struggled to be free of him. He moved so that only his head lay on her breast.

'Dear God,' he said, his mouth on her skin, 'it's been fifteen years.'

'Tell me,' she said with an impulse of tenderness that made her stroke his hair.

It was the story of a marriage that would not have lasted

five years had he been in any other profession.

'It was my fault,' he told her. 'I should never have married her, but I loved her. At least I suppose I loved her. I find it hard to remember how I felt at that time. If I'd been wiser I would have realised . . .' he broke off with a sigh.

'A colleague of mine who was courting at the same time used to talk endlessly about his fiancée, her passionate nature, how he had to put the brake on every time they went out together and how hard it was. I used to congratulate myself somewhat smugly on choosing the sort of woman who would hardly let me embrace her when we were officially engaged. I was proud of her purity and thankful for it. I was not like my colleague. I could not have put the brakes on like he did. I was afraid of the tiger within me and I felt that my salvation lay with someone like Joan. I was prepared to wait till we were married. It was not her fault that I . . .'

He twisted away impatiently. 'But why should you be interested?' he said harshly. 'It's no business of yours.'

'Of course I'm interested,' she said, but it was not altogether true. Her interest was only in his body. As he turned back to her she knew that she wanted him again.

'Even on our honeymoon,' he continued, 'I admired her for her modesty in certain matters. But as the weeks passed, I began to suspect that something was wrong. To begin with, I thought it was my fault, that I had hurt her or misbehaved in some unforgivable way. It took me years to realise that she was born without whatever it is that makes women want men. We began to quarrel and she made it quite clear that she thought the whole business of sex degrading, even disgusting. She only put up with it because she felt it was her duty to provide me with a child. But there was no child. She went to the doctor but apparently there

99

was nothing wrong with her. Then I happened to mention to the doctor that I'd had a bad go of mumps as a boy.'

' "That probably accounts for it, then," he said, and explained what mumps could do to adolescent boys.

'I told Joan that night. I expected recriminations and I would not have blamed her if she had been upset. I was disappointed myself, but she took it very well. Looking back, I can see she was relieved. Childbirth has always disgusted her. Shortly afterwards she got 'flu or some trivial ailment and I moved into another room. I've been there ever since.'

'It must have been hard for you,' she told him, but she was only half concentrating. She turned on her side towards him and slowly began to trace the outline of his face with her fingers.

'Harder than you can ever know,' he replied, so engrossed in his memories that he did not appear to notice her caressing hands. 'For a while I wanted every woman I met. Every night my bed was a battle-ground where I fought my dreams and lusts. I was at war with the whole female sex. I'm afraid I earned something of a reputation for rudeness.'

'So I've noticed,' she said softly, moving her hand from his face to his neck and shoulders.

'I thought I'd conquered that part of my nature. Women haven't disturbed me for years. I believed I was beyond it. And then,' he added, turning to her and drawing her closer while she smoothed and stroked his back, 'you caught me off-guard. I don't really know why I telephoned Kenneth to offer you a lift. I don't think we have spoken to each other more than half a dozen times, but you've always interested me, you and your family. Five sons! I should have liked five sons. I would have been content with one.' He paused and her hand slid down, pressing and kneading the small of his back. 'Then we climbed that hill together and I realised that I was falling in love like a ridiculous immature adolescent.'

But she had stopped listening. He was so different from Ken, whose body had a certain fragility. The Dean was altogether stronger, harder, heavier under her hand as she caressed and explored. He drew her against him, responding to her touch, yet still wanting to talk, to explain, to marvel at what had happened.

'They all told me at the meeting that I was mad to attempt the journey home with snow forecast, but I thought the sooner I returned home to my normal duties the sooner I could put you out of my thoughts.' He was breathing fast, the words coming in breathless gasps. 'Deep down I suppose I hoped this would happen, but believe me, I would not have touched you if you hadn't shown me that you cared.'

'You talk too much,' she whispered, moving on top of him, her mouth covering his.

She came almost as soon as he penetrated, a shuddering exquisite climax that made her cry out, and yet when it was over and she lay inert and totally relaxed, there was no familiar sense of contentment. It was almost as if she had had sex with herself, a solo performance in which she had taken what she could get and given nothing in return. When he spoke, she started.

'Thank you, my very dearest, for your wonderful love.'

That word again and this time it chilled her. Love and lust were strictly divisible as Jim had said only the day before. She did not want the Dean's love. It was too strong, too intense and would soon become unmanageable. She had shared her body with him to their mutual enjoyment. That was enough. He began to stroke her hair and she had the urge to brush his hand away like a persistent fly.

'I don't feel that we have done wrong. Does that sound blasphemous? We have committed adultery, but I have absolutely no sense of guilt.'

It was different for her. Not that she felt any sense of guilt towards his God; nor even towards her husband. She had given away nothing that she could not afford. She had not given at all, she had merely taken. Her guilt was directed entirely towards the Dean for whom at this moment she could only feel irritation.

'What are we going to do?' he asked.

'Do?' she replied, not attempting to hide her impatience. 'We're going to try and get some sleep.'

Leaning on his elbow he looked down at her and touched her cheek. 'I scarcely dare sleep in case I wake up and find you gone.'

She could sense his deep inner joy. His happiness lay like a load on her own heart.

'I won't go away,' she told him with a sigh.

II

He slept almost as soon as he closed his eyes, his exhausted body heavy against hers. She shifted, trying to avoid his weight, but she could not escape the burden of sadness that was beginning to press on her heart. She had been a virgin when she married and she had remained a loyal wife for twenty-odd years. She had allowed a stranger access to what had been private property and though she could not believe that his presence there had spoiled the property, somehow it had changed it in so far as it was no longer private. It was all so unfair, she thought bitterly. Other people slept around without experiencing this dreary aftermath of regret.

At last she fell into an unhappy doze which must have been heavier than she thought for when she awoke it was morning, and she was alone in bed.

Morning in the mountains was dazzling. Snow reflecting from the frosted mounds turned the light white. The interior of the bedroom was so bright that she could see dust rising slowly on a shaft of sunlight that had forced its way through a gap in the thin cotton curtains. She felt sticky and uncomfortable and she had a headache. The memory of what had happened still lay like a load on her heart, but after she had washed in the minute bathroom under the stairs, she began to feel better. She was brushing her hair when the Dean knocked on the door and came in carrying a tray.

'So you're awake,' he said cheerfully. 'Mrs Beck thought you might like some tea.'

She looked at him in surprise. His eyes were clear, he had a good colour and he was smiling. He put the tea on the chest of drawers and came over to her, putting his arms round her waist and drawing her close to him in a movement that was both gentle and protective.

'How are you this morning, dearest?' he asked. 'Did you sleep well?'

He bent to kiss her mouth, but she moved her head so that his lips brushed her hair.

'What are the roads like?' she asked, freeing herself from his grasp. 'Will we able to get home?'

'Beck and I have cleared a path to the car. He says the snow-plough should be through at any moment,' he said, drawing back the curtains so that the full force of the sun flooded over them. 'It's a splendid morning. Come and see.'

She moved to the window reluctantly. He was right. The air was fresh and pure; everything that she was not. He put his arm round her shoulders.

'Do you recognise where we are?'

It was only a mile or so from the track they had explored on the journey down, and she knew that he too was remembering the story of the girl who had gone mad with love; but on this sharp white morning, the tale held no romance for her. The thought of love depressed her unreasonably. Suddenly she shivered.

'You're cold,' he said, drawing her close to him so that her head rested stiffly on his shoulder. 'No wonder. I'll leave you to get dressed, but don't be long. Mrs Beck is preparing another gargantuan feast.'

'Oh Lord,' she said, 'I'm not in the least hungry.'

He laughed. 'Fortunately, I am.'

She dressed quickly and packed her overnight bag. Then she tidied the little room and took off the sheets, folding them carefully and putting them on the chest of drawers. With any luck she would not have to come upstairs again. In the kitchen, Mr Beck, a tough little man as wrinkled as an old apple, and the Dean were bent over steaming mounds of porridge. The Dean stood up as she came in and Mrs Beck fussed about her lack of appetite. She felt it was ungracious to refuse the lavish portions of bacon and egg sizzling on the stove, but the thought of food still sickened her. She drank two cups of tea and ate some bread while the Dean and Beck compared notes on mountaineering. He laughed a great deal and talked more amusingly than she had thought him capable of doing, but his good spirits had an edge of irresponsibility that worried her, and she longed to escape.

'There goes t'plough,' said Mr Beck, moving to the window and looking out at the noisy vehicle on the road outside. 'You'll get home soon enough now.'

'Fortunately we're in no particular hurry,' said the Dean, buttering some more bread.

'What made you say that?' Alison asked almost angrily when the Becks were out of earshot.

The Dean looked up in surprise at the sharpness of her tone.

'We've a great deal to talk about,' he said reasonably.

'For heaven's sake, let's get on our way. Besides,' she added impatiently, 'we can't possibly talk here.'

If only, she thought, smoothing her headachey brow and avoiding his puzzled eyes, if only he would say nothing, the previous night could be forgotten. It could be as if it had never happened.

'Look,' she said, trying to sound conciliatory, 'can't we just go home?'

He said nothing, but she was thankful to see that he did not try to delay their departure in spite of Mrs Beck's entreaties. He drove slowly and carefully over the hard-packed snow, and for a while she thought that he was not going to say anything more, but once they had got through the mountains he stopped in a lay-by close to a wood. The snow was not so deep here, but the little Christmas trees were trimmed with white and under them the snow was creased and crossed with the marks of birds and small animals while the sun slanted across the road casting dark intricate shadows. It was a fairy-tale world, but she felt no part of it. He turned to her and she was suddenly afraid.

'Alison, dearest, I have the feeling that – like me – you want to postpone making any major decisions, but we have to consider what we are going to do.'

'Why should we have to do anything?' she said sullenly.

'Life can never be quite the same again for either of us. Surely you see that?'

'Of course it can,' she insisted stubbornly. Fear added an edge to her voice. 'You're married; I'm married. Nothing can change that.'

He started to put his arm round her, but when she moved to the corner of the seat he did not persist.

'You may be right, but at the same time, after what happened last night, our marriages can never be the same.'

He was making such a production out of it.

'Nothing happened last night,' she said, her voice rising. 'We were in the mood so we had sex. What could be simpler than that? Our bodies were involved for a few hours but nothing else. Don't you understand?'

He was silent for a moment.

'No,' he said at length, 'I don't think I do.'

'Look,' she said wearily, 'don't you think we should just go home? I'd like to find a phone-box to ring Ken as soon as possible and I daresay your wife will be worried too.'

'In a moment,' he said firmly. 'First I must know what you propose to tell Kenneth . . .'

'When to come and meet me, of course,' she said impatiently.

'. . . about what happened last night,' he continued as if she had not spoken.

'I keep telling you as far as I'm concerned, nothing happened last night.'

'As far as you're concerned, maybe,' he repeated with a touch of asperity, 'but you are not the only one concerned. I am concerned and your husband is concerned whether you like it or not.'

She shook her head. 'You're wrong. Ken could only be concerned if he knew and the same applies to your wife. I don't propose to tell either of them. Do you?'

She saw that she had shocked him.

'Look,' she said, turning to him. 'Confession may be good for one's soul, but it can do a hell of a lot of harm to other people. I love Ken too much to make him a sop to my pathetic conscience. I have a good marriage and I don't want it harmed.'

'Isn't it a little late to think of that?'

'Why should it be? I haven't harmed Ken or our marriage. I haven't given away anything of value. I could afford it.'

'Then you don't love me,' he said quietly.

'Love,' she said despairingly. 'Love is too big a thing to be given away so lightly. Love-making and love are not necessarily synonymous.'

'So what happened between us last night meant nothing to you?' he asked incredulously.

'Of course it meant something at the time, but not in the scheme of our lives, no more and no less than any other satisfying experience . . . and even if we had fallen in love with each other, what difference would it make? Divorce is out of the question as far as we are concerned. We are too old, too involved with the pattern of our lives to behave like irresponsible teenagers. Can't we accept last night for what it was and get on with the business of living?'

There was a note of desperation in her voice, as if she were trying to convince herself as well as him.

'You make it sound very easy.'

'It is easy,' she said eagerly, 'if only you will allow it to be.'

'For you perhaps.'

She wanted to say something soft, something gentle and encouraging, but she could not find the words. She was in a fever to be home, to reassure herself that all she had told the Dean was true. She was also afraid. If she were to turn to him now, comfort him, take him in her arms, she might find that her careful excuses and reasonings had become meaningless.

'Look,' she began hesitatingly, 'I blame myself . . .'

'I understand,' he said curtly. 'There's nothing more to be said.'

Eventually he started the car and they drove in complete silence for the rest of the journey. An hour later they reached the hotel. She looked quickly round the car-park for a sign of Ken and saw with relief that he had not yet arrived to take her home.

'Don't wait,' she told the Dean when he had helped her into the hotel with her parcels. 'Ken may be another half-hour at least, and I expect you're anxious to get home.'

She knew her voice sounded false and formal, but she desperately wanted him to go. She needed a few minutes of peace to calm herself and prepare for Ken.

'As you like,' he said, and turned away.

She could not bear the closed cold look in his eyes.

'George,' she called after him.

He stopped but did not turn. She went up to him. If the receptionist had not been there, she would have kissed him to make the peace between them. Instead she held out her hand.

'I'm sorry,' she said, 'for my inadequacies, for hurting you, for not living up to your image of me, for making you sin.' It was all in her eyes if only he had looked to see.

'Yes,' he said, without touching her, and left the hotel.

She stood at the lounge window and watched him go. This was the moment she had been waiting for all morning, but now that it had come, she realised that his going solved nothing. What will become of him? she thought, as she watched his grey and unsmiling figure cross to the car-park, and at the same moment she was swept by the old familiar yearning ache. For one wild moment she wanted to run after him, put her arms round him and tell him what he wanted to hear.

Dear God, she thought as she turned from the window. She did not know what she wanted.

12

She had time to wash and drink some coffee before Ken arrived. Sitting at a table in the window, she watched him park the car and walk towards the hotel. Partly because of her recent experience and partly because she had not seen him for a couple of days, she found herself looking at him with sharp perceptive eyes. It was the first time she had looked at him with curiosity for years, and what she saw moved her with compassion. He looked so thin; thin-haired, thin-boned. His clothes hung on him. Although not yet fifty, he seemed an old man. Apart from the physical changes there was something else indefinably different about him. In spite of his familiar features and the clothes she knew as well as her own, he seemed like a stranger. With dismay, she realised that if he were strange to her, it must be she who had made him so. He was the same man who had married her and fathered her children. It was her eyes, her heart, her mind that saw him differently. She was the stranger, not he.

She stood up as he came into the lounge and moved towards him, eager to reassure herself that all was well between them, that nothing had changed. She put her hands on his shoulders and embraced him in a proprietorial manner.

'There you are then,' he said, stiffening in her embrace. She dropped her arms, chilled by his reception until she remembered that Ken had always hated a public show of feelings. She had learned not to be demonstrative in public. His rejection of her welcome was in character. It was no different from any other greeting between them, or so she told herself as he began to pick up her parcels.

'Is this everything?' he asked.

'I think so,' she said, giving a last look round.

The receptionist nodded to them and the porter held open the door as they left the hotel. Her smile made her mouth feel stiff.

'How have you managed?' she asked as they settled in the car.

'Well enough,' he replied non-committally.

He did not mention her journey and nor did she. Everything relevant had already been said when she had phoned him from a call-box just outside the town.

'How is everything in the village?' she asked, wanting him to join her in the normality of inconsequential conversation.

'Much as usual, I believe.'

Chilled by his non-communicativeness, she could not be sure whether he was acting normally or whether she was expecting more from him than he was accustomed to give. She had a moment of panic when she found she could not remember what he was really like. She felt she did not know him at all, as if the twenty years had counted for nothing. Firmly she tried to tell herself that he was just the same as he always was.

'I had lunch with the Sharpes yesterday,' she told him, determined to share all she could with him.

He did not reply.

'Don't you want to hear about them?' she asked. Her frayed nerves made her sound irritable.

'Whether or not I'm interested is beside the point. You intend to tell me.'

It was a typical reply of his and one which in the past she had regarded as a humorous invitation for her to go ahead. Now she was not so certain. In her new state of critical perception she thought she detected an edge to his voice.

'Margaret's pregnant and Martin and Brenda seem to think it's the end of the world,' she said, allowing a faint sneer to come into her tone.

'Perhaps it is – for them,' he replied quietly.

'Oh Ken, really!' In the light of her own adultery she needed to belittle Margaret's. 'You're as bad as they are.'

'Perhaps that's what's wrong with the world today. Too many people think the old values and moralities don't matter.'

'Well, but do they matter all that much?' she asked argumentatively.

'I believe they do.'

She was silent, depressed by his inflexibility. If only he could unbend a little, she would be comforted. Yet, she told herself, why should he change his standards because she had lowered hers? She did not want him to do so. Had she not often told herself that as long as he stuck to his principles, it did not matter what she did? She still thought the same way, and yet, if he could have shown a scrap of tenderness towards her at that moment, she could more easily have borne the weight of her depression and guilt.

There was little snow by the coast. A thin sprinkle covered the fields, but the road was clear and a sluggish sea pushed dully away at the shingle. The village lay ahead of them snug in its sheltering bay, but for the first time her heart did not lift at the sight of it. It had a shut-in closed aspect that made her think of prison.

'Are there any letters from the boys?' she asked suddenly

as the thought came into her head. Normally it was the first question she would have asked.

'I believe there's one,' he replied.

'Don't you know?' she asked incredulously.

'The post only arrived as I left.'

She had always known that hers was the most obvious interest where the boys were concerned, but up till now she had always believed his affection for them to be at least as strong as hers. Now she was even beginning to doubt that.

'Why didn't you bring it with you?' she demanded, close to tears.

But she knew it was no use blaming him for lack of interest in his sons. She herself had not given them a thought for the past twenty-four hours.

'It won't run away,' he said mildly.

For the first time he sounded like the Ken she knew and she was temporarily reassured.

'Do you want to stop in the village for anything?' he asked presently as they reached the outskirts.

He did not seem to know what was left in the larder so she asked to be let off at the main store. As she got out of the car, Mrs Smiley, an energetic church member, came beaming towards her.

'I'm glad you're back safely, dear. May I run round one morning to talk about the Daffodil Coffee Morning?'

Alison let her talk for a few minutes and then escaped into the village shop. It was crowded as usual at this hour of the morning. Most of the villagers dropped in during the course of the day to pick up local news or alleviate loneliness. They all greeted her with the customary comments on the weather or queries about her sons, and she had a sudden image of herself thirty years hence still standing in the same shop listening to the same comments. Her hair would be white and she would probably have arthritis, the occupational disease of parsons' wives, but otherwise nothing would be changed. She had a sudden wild desire to smash everything within reach. Was it always like this? Were the villagers always so provincial? Was her life always so dull? Up till now she had been content. But now . . .

Her head was throbbing and her limbs ached. She knew she was tired. One thing was certain. She was not going to let a commonplace act of adultery ruin the rest of her life. She would be herself in a day or two. It was no wonder she felt as she did after such a night. She was all right really. Everything was going to be all right.

She forced herself to walk jauntily back to the car.

The parsonage smelled of damp and old age. There was a film of dust on the hall table and there was the letter from her youngest son. She picked it up as Ken brought in the parcels and her case. She looked at the handwriting. Its unformed childishness moved her unbearably. She had blamed Ken in her heart for not having had sufficient interest to open it, but now, for some reason, she could not open it either. She put it in her pocket and went through to the kitchen to prepare a meal. She heard the study door close.

It was not until the afternoon that she could bring herself to open the letter.

Dear Mum and Dad,

We've had lots of snow and I've been sledging a bit. One of the boys smashed into a tree. It will never be the same again – the tree, I mean! ! The snow was so bad that we were snowed up yesterday so I didn't get any letters and so I thought I would write instead. Is my cider OK? I wonder if Duguld is OK in this weather.

Would you have a look and see? Please let me know at once. With lots of love . . .

Duguld was the tortoise who had gone into winter hibernation in a box in the tool-shed before Christmas, but Alison knew that he was not her child's primary concern. He was homesick. The first excitement of the new life had worn off and he was feeling very much the little boy in a strange environment. She re-read the letter and tears filled her eyes as she looked at the word 'love'. But she was not weeping for her son, at least not altogether. She was remembering the Dean as she had last seen him after that dreadful drive home. She remembered how he had looked as he had left her and all her grief was for him. There was no room left in her heart for anyone else, not even her son.

On her way upstairs she paused at the study door. For twenty years she had shared her problems, her griefs and disappointments with Ken. Trivial little worries such as the time she had called the Bishop's wife a battle-axe in her hearing; not such trivial matters as when her third son had failed most of his O-levels; and serious matters as when her parents had died so tragically so close one after the other. Ken had always been the first to know and the first to comfort her. Now she had an acute longing to share this final burden with him. If she could tell him everything right from the start, she would find relief and comfort even in his scorn and anger.

But she could not do it. This time she had to stand alone. She would have to bear the burden of guilt, her disloyalty and her cruelty by herself. She passed the study door and went upstairs alone. She went into the room she shared with him, she lay on the bed she shared with him, but she had to weep by herself.

13

Flowering currant and pussy-willow bloomed in the large winter-tidy garden. A brisk March wind blew Alison's hair across her face as she pruned the thorn-straggly rose bushes. Fading aconites with enlarged green ruffs drooped between the purple and white crocus spires and the leggy remnants of snowdrops. Alison put a rose clipping in the wheel-barrow and watched a blackbird quarrel with a starling over an unprotesting worm. She spent a great deal of time in the garden now, more time than she spent in the house. Here she did not have to think.

Clem's white Viva swept up the drive and crunched to a halt outside the front door of the vicarage. Instinctively, Alison moved behind the sheltering trunk of a horse-chestnut tree. She hoped Clem would go away when she found that the house was empty, and waited, tense, to hear the start of the engine.

'There you are!' Clem exclaimed, coming into the garden. 'What on earth are you doing skulking behind a tree?'

Alison flushed with guilt and annoyance.

'Why should you think I'm skulking?'

'At least you have the grace to blush.'

Clem came over, hatless and laughing in the breezy air. She looked so cheerful and uncomplicated that Alison envied her.

'Admit it now, you've been avoiding me for weeks, and

not only me. Mrs Smiley is in a panic over the Daffodil Coffee Morning. Not that I blame you for dodging behind bushes when she comes to call, but I resent it on my own behalf.'

Alison smiled faintly.

'Well, that's better,' Clem said ironically. 'And now do you think you could spare me half an hour from your gardening? My beloved little Honey is having his coat clipped.'

Alison led the way into the house. The hall had a dusty uncared-for look, and there was a patch of dried mud on the carpet that had been there for days. The kitchen smelled stale and the sink was piled with the lunch dishes.

'Mrs Bews comes tomorrow,' she said by way of excuse, but she could see that Clem was surprised.

Alison's kitchen, usually bright with flowers and warm with the gleaming white Esse, had, until lately, been one of the gathering places for the village. Here she had dispensed coffee and advice with home-made cakes and gossip. She put on the kettle and found a few stale biscuits while listening without comment to Clem's inconsequential village chatter.

'And now,' said Clem, waving away the nasty biscuits, but accepting a mug of tea, 'it's your turn. Some explanations first, if you please. What's happened, Alison?'

'Happened?' Alison frowned and turned away to avoid the probing eyes of her friend. 'Nothing's happened. What should have happened?'

'That's what I came to find out. You haven't been yourself for a long time, not since the end of the Christmas holidays.'

Alison grasped the proffered straw.

'I miss the children,' she said quickly. 'The house is so quiet and dull, I can hardly bear it.'

'I don't believe you,' Clem said seriously. 'If you found the house as quiet and dull as you say it is, you would make excuses to get out of it. As it is, you skulk – there's no other word for it – behind doors as well as bushes. In the name of God, why?'

It was true, of course. There was no point in denying it. When Ken was out, she refused to answer the door or the telephone. When her friends came right into the house and called her name at the foot of the stairs or in the kitchen, she would hide behind the bathroom door and hope they would not hear her breathing. How could she begin to explain to Clem that she had lost all interest in living? Nothing was the same, and yet, basically, nothing had changed. Ken was much as he had always been, perhaps a little quieter, a little more withdrawn, but this she blamed on herself. She was not much fun to be with these days. She still wrote regularly and heard from her sons, but now it took her all her time to make her letters interesting, and she no longer watched for the postman.

Her work in the parish, never much at the best of times, dwindled to nothing. She began to cut church services, pleading headaches. The several old people who had looked forward to her visits were left to wonder how they had offended the vicar's wife, and the wool for the Mission Knitters was not yet distributed. Life had become a relentless pulse of hours to be endured. But how to tell Clem?

She knew her present state of mind must be because of what had happened with the Dean, and yet, looking back at the affair logically, she could see no reason why her whole life should be spoiled because of an act that had lasted only one night; an act of self-gratification which should have had no more drastic effect than eating a box of chocolates or drinking too much wine.

Her brain told her that she had done nothing wrong, except in so far as she had hurt the Dean's pride or feelings, and yet as she lay sleepless beside her husband she still longed to tell him everything, to weep and beg his forgiveness. Forgiveness for what? she would ask herself. She did not believe she had done him any harm. Why should she risk hurting him to relieve her own feelings? Ken at least should be spared.

But there was something that Ken could not be spared. He would have to know sooner or later.

'Alison,' Clem nudged her from her thoughts.

'I'm pregnant,' she said at last.

Clem breathed out quickly. 'So that's it. Actually I did wonder. But why the gloom . . .'

'My eldest son is twenty . . .'

'So what? You're not forty yet. Considering how much you miss the boys, I should have thought you'd be delighted. It might even be a girl this time. What does Ken think?'

'He doesn't know, and for God's sake don't tell him,' she said hastily.

'Why ever not? I presume the child is his,' she said, laughing at the absurdity of the idea.

Alison turned her head away to hide the sudden rush of blood to her cheeks.

'Just don't, that's all. I'll tell him myself when the moment comes. I'm not at all certain yet myself. I've only missed twice.'

Conclusive enough, nevertheless, she thought. She had not missed a period since her last pregnancy thirteen years ago. She knew it was true, and that she must begin to make decisions. The dreaded question to be faced was whether to tell Ken all of what she believed to be the truth, or live with the lie for the rest of her life.

Clem stood up and came over to her.

'Cheer up, darling. This baby will be the brightest and most beautiful of them all. You'll see.'

She left almost immediately and Alison was alone once again with her problem. It would have to be faced now. Whether or not Ken was the father of her unborn child, he had the right to know that she was pregnant. It was just possible that the child was his. They both knew that the safe period was not reliable. Yet why, after thirteen years, should this method which had proved reliable in their case, suddenly go wrong? The child would be born in wedlock; legally it would be Ken's, but physically, she was sure it belonged to the Dean.

In spite of his childish ailment and his wife's barrenness, she was certain that it was his, as certain in her heart as she was that the other five were fathered by Ken. Could she give birth to this child and rear him while knowing that his brothers were not his brothers and his father not his father? It was a lie that would last a life-time and as yet she did not know how she would be able to live it. Yet the alternative was equally unthinkable. To tell Ken and the Dean what she suspected to be the case would be to disrupt all their lives. The Dean, she supposed, had some right to know, but whose rights took precedence?

She remembered how she had pitied Mary the loss of her womb. She had believed then that she could lose nothing more valuable than that which had sheltered her sons. Now she envied her. She would trade her womb for Mary's emptiness if she could.

Now that Clem knew about the child, she would have to tell Ken immediately. Clem could not be trusted to keep such a confidence, and by tomorrow the news would be all over the village. Poor Ken, she thought. Old maids would look at him slyly and lusty men would laugh. Oh Ken, she thought with anguish, how happy she would be if the child could be proved to be his.

He was late in getting home that evening for there had been a clergy meeting in Coolwater Bay. She could see he was tired. She had made an effort with the evening meal and she felt ready to talk to him.

They ate in the kitchen with the rusty cat called Horrible snoring in the basket chair.

'Clem came,' she told him as she ladled soup into two brown pots.

'Oh yes?' he said absently, glancing at the letters which had come by the afternoon post. 'Did she tell you how Mary is?'

'How awful,' she exclaimed, 'I forgot to ask.'

'Awful?' Ken frowned. 'Awe-full?' he repeated. 'Thoughtless, possibly, but not surprising.'

She knew he was tired. Quibbling at her misuse of language was a sure sign.

'I had something important on my mind,' she told him by way of excuse.

He crossed himself and started to drink the soup.

'Aren't you interested?'

'In what?'

It seemed to her that he was being particularly obtuse, but it was typical of their conversations these days.

'In what I'm trying to tell you.' She forced herself to be reasonable.

'That rather depends.'

'Depends on what?'

A skin had formed on her soup. She lifted it carefully with the back of her spoon.

'On whether or not it concerns me.'

'Well, of course it concerns you.' Lying was easier, she found, when you shouted. 'I'm going to have a baby.'

His expression did not change, but it seemed to her that he grew a shade paler.

'I was wondering when you were going to tell me.'

'How did you know?'

'I haven't lived through five of your pregnancies without knowing something of the way they affect you.'

'Am I always like this?' she asked, wonderingly.

'Let's say you are not at your sparkling best.'

He smiled faintly, and she could see that he was making an effort to be kind. She reached across the table and took his hand.

'Oh Ken,' she said, 'I'm so glad you know. I don't feel so awful – badly . . .' she corrected herself quickly, 'about it now.'

It was almost as if she had told him the whole truth. Relief made her garrulous. It became easier and easier.

'Of course I'm not absolutely sure. It seems so unfair when we've always been so careful.'

'There was always a risk,' he said quietly.

'I know,' she agreed eagerly, drinking her soup in quick gulps. 'That's what the books say. Perhaps I should have taken the pill, but we never got round to discussing it, did we?'

He said nothing, but she did not notice his sudden withdrawal of attention.

'What will the boys say, do you think? Will they be horrified?'

He stood up and went into the pantry.

'It would be nice if it were a girl this time,' she called after him.

She picked up her empty soup bowl and followed him

into the pantry. He was leaning over the sink and holding the taps for support.

'What's wrong, darling? Aren't you well?'

'I feel a little sick, that's all. It will pass.'

He looked ghastly.

'Is it the soup?' she asked, full of concern.

'No, no,' he said impatiently. 'It was probably that pie I had in the snack bar at the station for lunch. It's nothing, I tell you.'

'Go to bed and I'll bring you a hot bottle. You look really rotten.'

'Oh, don't fuss so. I'm perfectly all right.' He came back into the kitchen, white as whey. 'I've got some work to do. Don't wait up for me. I'll probably be late.'

'Are you sure?' she asked doubtfully.

Looking at him closely, she was anxious for him. It seemed to her that he had not been himself for some time. His appetite, never robust, was pitiable at the moment. He was always in his study working when not out on his parish rounds. But she had been so wrapped up in her own thoughts that she had not till now noticed how wretched he looked.

'I do wish you would go to bed and let me bring you something, darling,' she said, anxiously.

He seemed to shrink from her warmth.

'I'm just a little tired, that's all. I had to chair the meeting.'

'I thought the Dean was chairman . . .' She broke off, surprised at the ease with which she spoke of him.

'So he is – when he's there. At the moment he's in hospital.'

'Hospital?' she echoed.

'Surely you knew. He's had some sort of breakdown. He's been in Lethey Bridge for over a month now,' he added as he picked up his letters and left the room.

14

It had nothing to do with her, she tried to tell herself over and over again as she cleared the table and washed the supper dishes. The Dean had been heading for a breakdown for months. Martin had said so, and she had thought it herself on at least one occasion. It was the inevitable result of overwork, an incompatible marriage and his own temperament. It had nothing to do with her.

She turned on both taps and began to scour the lustreless steel sink. She remembered how Ken had stood there, grey and nauseated, just after she had told him about the child. She wondered if there could be a connection. Needled with anxiety, nevertheless she was convinced that Ken suspected nothing. He was tired just as he had explained, and his cool manner was accounted for by her difficult behaviour over the past two months. She knew she had not been easy to live with. There had been little companionship between them. It occurred to her that there had never been much companionship between them even in the early days of their marriage. It had not mattered when she had had her children round her. Now it was glaringly obvious. But Ken was not a man who needed companionship. Why should she expect him to behave differently now? It was neurotic to start worrying about that. Had not Ken himself given her the perfect excuse for her behaviour by putting it down to her pregnancy? The Dean's illness was, however, a matter which she could not put so easily out of her mind. Suppose she were responsible for his breakdown, it would not be the first time she had helped to drive a man out of his mind.

She had not thought about that particular affair for years; the memory of it was still shocking to her, but now, like the Ancient Mariner, she found she had to re-live it step by painful step.

She had been married for just over a year and her first baby was still at her breast. Ken was on his last tour as a Naval Chaplain and she was on her way to join him. The troopship was overcrowded and she had to share a cabin with half a dozen other wives. After leaving her baby asleep in the string cot slung to her bunk, she escaped from the noisy nappy-slung cabin on the first morning at sea and found her way up to the boat deck.

At that hour the upper deck was practically empty. A man in white shorts was doing push-ups by the life-boats. Close by, a middle-aged man in civilian clothes was sitting alone. His thin hair lifted slightly in the fresh morning breeze and the sun shone on his pale anxious face. Insecure and friendless herself, she began to talk to him. He told her he was one of the few civilians on the ship and on his way to a new job and a new life abroad. He was an unprepossessing little man with the beginnings of a paunch, but he was someone with whom to share the early morning loneliness. For the next few mornings they had long conversations and he showed her photographs of his wife and children in their drab Midlands home. When they parted for breakfast – they had different dining-room sittings – she saw no more of him and indeed forgot his existence. She made a number of new friends among the officers and wives of her own age group with similar interests. He meant less than nothing to her. She never even knew his surname.

After a week, however, they were still meeting in the early

morning, and his conversation began to take on a more personal note; also he began to seek her out during the day. Her friends made no secret of the fact that they regarded him as a bore, and she, being young and impressionable, soon began to see him in a similar light. He was always hanging about waiting for her at the entrance to one of the lounges or on deck, and, when he approached, her more amusing friends drifted away.

One day, exasperated to anger by his proprietary attitude, she turned on him. She still remembered the words, for shame had etched them on her memory.

'For God's sake stop creeping about after me like a sick dog. Why won't you leave me alone?'

'I thought we were friends.' His unconfident eyes were reproachful.

'Whatever gave you that idea?'

She turned and ran from him towards the retreating backs of her friends. That night, after giving her child his evening feed, she hurried back to the boat deck where she had left her friends watching the moon rise over a phosphorescent sea. He must have been waiting for her at the top of the gangway, for he darted out of the shadows, and, catching her arm, pulled her into a dark corner.

'I've got to speak to you,' he said, breathing rapidly. She was sickeningly aware of his sexual excitement.

'Let me go,' she demanded, writhing in his grasp.

'Not until you tell me why you've been avoiding me. What have I done? Am I not good enough for you and your fine friends? Is that it?'

'For heaven's sake!' she said scornfully.

'That's it, isn't it! You think I'm no good at it. I'll show you. I'll effing well show you.'

He pressed her back against the rail. His hot wet lips

slobbered on her face as they groped towards her mouth in the dark. His breath smelled of onions. She was revolted.

'You're disgusting!' she cried, twisting her head away. 'You absolutely disgust me.'

He released her then and as she left him standing there she could not tell whether he was panting or sobbing.

She never saw him again.

She spent the first few days after the encounter avoiding him, but it was at least a week before she realised he was not around any more. The boat deck in the early morning was crowded now with passengers gasping the cool early breeze, so that had he been there, she might easily have missed him. She might not have noticed his absence at all if one of her friends had not said to her while they were waiting to play deck quoits: 'Whatever happened to that odd little man in the hot clothes who used to follow you about?'

Out of curiosity, she kept her eyes open for a couple of days. One of her friends who attended the same dining-room sitting reported he had not been in his place for at least a week.

'Probably seasick,' said someone.

'What, in this calm?' Alison queried, thinking it was probably just the sort of spineless thing that would happen to him.

That night, because she had nothing better to do, she asked one of his cabin-mates what had become of the little civilian. He was a foreigner of sorts and a very attractive man, but he was not a mixer and secretly she had been sorry for she had felt that his friendship was more worth having than any of her other acquaintances. It was therefore partly to satisfy her curiosity and partly to wangle from him an invitation to have a drink at the bar, that she made a point of speaking to him.

'Whatever happened to your civilian cabin-mate?' she asked. 'I haven't seen him around for a while.'

'Are you really interested?' he asked her coldly.

'Of course I'm interested.'

'Then I'll tell you, but not to gratify your curiosity. I'm going to tell you because I think it's about time you grew up. I hope you are still young enough to learn for I'm going to teach you a lesson you'll never forget.'

She saw with dismay that he was really angry. A little afraid, she turned away, unwilling to hear more.

'Listen,' he said roughly. 'Your friend is in sick bay. He tried to take his own life by slashing his wrists. It was fortunate he was found in time.'

She had to hold on to the rails. 'I'm sorry of course, but I can't see what it's got to do with me.'

'You were warned, were you not, as were the rest of us, what effect the tropics can have on sexual relationships? You must have seen how attracted he was to you. Unless you were completely blind you must have seen how homesick and unhappy he was.'

'I suppose so.'

'And yet you still ask what it has got to do with you!' He lowered his voice. His eyes were steel blue knives. 'You deliberately set out to make that man want you. I watched you posturing on deck.'

'That's not true!' she cried.

'Isn't it? He had a wife whom he loved and peace of mind until you came into his life. You hurt that man; you hurt him so badly that he no longer wanted to go on living. There is a name for women like you – cock-teaser.'

He turned and left her shocked to the soul. For years that conversation haunted her. Even though, as she grew older, she realised the sailor probably had hang-ups of his own, and was not the judgement of God personified, it made no difference to the shame and guilt she experienced whenever she remembered. And now, after so many years, it looked as if history had repeated itself. Just as she had driven the little civilian to want to die, she had driven the Dean to the limits of endurance.

But I'm not like that, she cried inwardly. She had always regarded herself as a virtuous woman – 'a follower of godly matrons' – as it said so delightfully in the marriage service, whose love was only towards her husband and sons. She had done wrong according to the book of rules, but why should her sin have consequences out of all proportion to its size? She remembered having read somewhere that in the hands of the virtuous, sin was a deadly weapon, but how unfair that was. If the Dean had allowed himself to fall in love with her that was his misfortune; it was no more her responsibility than the attempted suicide of the randy little civilian. Why should she feel responsible?

Thus her mind went round in circles trying to find a way round the mountain of responsibility. On her way to bed, she half thought of going into the study and asking Ken for further details of the Dean's breakdown, but as she passed his door, she heard him on the telephone, and carried on upstairs alone.

When Ken eventually came to bed, she was still awake. She reached out in the dark for his body. Desperate for warmth and reassurance, she pressed her breasts to his back and slid her hands under his pyjama jacket. It was something she had not done for months. She had not felt in the mood for intercourse lately and on the few occasions when he had wanted her, she had either pretended to be asleep or submitted to his embrace with the minimum of response. Therefore she could not blame him for not re-

sponding to her now. Partly she was disappointed for intercourse had always been best between them during her
pregnancies when there were no dates to remember or nag-
ging doubts and worries. Mostly, however, she was relieved.
She did not really desire him any more than he wanted her.

Ken turned away and moved on to his back. 'By the way,'
he said, 'I shall be going away for a few days. The conductor
at Bellfield Monastery rang tonight to say he had had a last-
minute cancellation for the retreat I had hoped to attend
this week.'

'When are you going?' she asked.

'Tomorrow. I'll be back late on Saturday night,' he told
her, 'all being well.'

She had forgotten that he always went to a retreat for
clergy round about this time of the year.

'Must you go?' The words were wrung from her out of
her confused state of mind and she sensed his surprise; by
this time, she knew better than to quibble over matters
concerning his spiritual life.

'Have you seen the doctor yet?' he asked, putting her
question down to anxiety over her pregnancy.

'The doctor?' she repeated stupidly.

'About the child.'

'No, not yet.'

'Then I think you should go to him as soon as possible.
You could be mistaken, you know.'

'Oh Ken, I'm not mistaken,' she said, feeling the tears
slide over her cheeks.

It was on the tip of her tongue to tell him then, to spill
out all the guilt and misery. She had even begun to arrange
the words she would use in her mind when he fell asleep.
As she listened to his sleep-breathing, she was drenched in
loneliness. The Dean's face haunted her dreams.

15

Now that she had come to Lethey Bridge, she was not at all sure of her motive. Certainly she had intended to visit Miss Taylor; she had intended to visit her for months now, for, up till Christmas, she had been Miss Taylor's sole visitor. The longer she evaded what she knew to be her duty the harder it became. Thus when she left Ken at the station, she had Miss Taylor both on her mind and on her conscience. She had taken the turning that led to the hills where Lethey Bridge was situated fully intending to go and see the old woman, but she knew Miss Taylor was not responsible for the quickening of her pulse and the nervous sweat on her palms.

At no time did she make a conscious decision to visit the Dean. Nevertheless when she came to the intersection in the corridor that separated the male from the female wards, she turned unhesitatingly towards the male section.

The quiet corridors of the hospital seemed to add to the dream-like quality of her act. Bright with pink light and red linoleum the long hot passages seemed to go on for ever. The further she walked the more distant the outside world became. She passed a number of cleaners – some of them long-term patients – swabbing the linoleum with disinfectant polish. Although they moved politely to let her pass, she had the feeling that they were as isolated from her and each other as coracles on an endless sea. The space that separated them had nothing to do with distance.

Ward Fifteen was a well-proportioned sunny room filled for the most part with senile old men sitting round a well-guarded open fire. She glanced through the glass partition in the door that opened into the annexe where she had been told she would find the Dean, and looked round quickly.

The square sitting-room was warmed by an open fire similar to the one in the main ward. A number of men were sitting in easy chairs, some reading, two playing chess; others sat quietly with their hands loose in their laps. The Dean was by the window.

The sight of him moved her more than she could have believed possible. It was like seeing someone as close to her as her father had been, after years of absence. She had forgotten how well she knew him, how familiar his features were. Although this sense of familiarity was unexpected, it was not unpleasant. She felt a stirring in her heart that might have been joy.

So intent had she been on his features and expression that she did not immediately see that his wife was with him. They were both looking out of the window with closed withdrawn expressions. A bag of fruit and some paperbacks, her sick-room offerings, lay on the occasional table between them. Her carefully arranged profile was inscrutable behind the discreet mask of make-up. At that moment she said something to her husband and stood up. A bright smile stretched her thin mouth and Alison could tell she was ill-at-ease in the hospital surroundings. She drew on her gloves and picked up her bag. The sight of the ordinary action brought Alison to her senses with a start. Although she had been standing there for barely a minute, it seemed like hours. She rubbed her palms against her coat as she turned reluctantly and went away.

Miss Taylor was very old and very senile. She had no

living relatives and not enough money to pay for private care, but she was not unhappy. She lived in a world peopled by her family and childhood friends. Patting the chair beside her in the long overcrowded ward sitting-room, she greeted Alison with a smile and a wildly inaccurate burst of recognition.

'What a time you've been, Cissy! I've been keeping this table for you all day. The café's very crowded, isn't it?'

Cissy had been her sister, dead for over twenty years.

Half listening to the long involved conversation of the old woman, Alison waited for the pulse of her heart to calm and her hands to stop trembling. She imagined the Dean's wife leaving the hospital on nervous clicking heels that jarred the peace of those quiet corridors. She saw her getting into the car, the same car that had taken them to Pendale. She saw her thin sharp shoulders relax in relief to be gone from the place and its problems. She saw with increasing dislike the tight mouth slacken a little, relieved that the burden of marriage which had become so impossible in recent weeks could be put aside for a few hours.

All at once she became aware of Miss Taylor. The little grey sparrow of a woman was angry.

'Sister, Sister!' she called in a quivering voice. 'Who is this person sitting at my table? Tell her to go away. She isn't my Cissy. I don't recognise her.'

The ward sister was by her side in a second, calming, coaxing, explaining. For a while, Miss Taylor glared at Alison, and then reassured by the protective arm of the nurse, her anger collapsed.

'I don't understand,' she said querulously. 'What is she doing here? Why has she come?'

The sister was apologetic, making excuses for the old woman on account of her age and senility, but to Alison there was a certain muddled logic behind the remarks, as if in some strange way, Miss Taylor had perceived the true state of her mind.

'It's all right,' she said, rising. 'I'll go now.'

'You'll come back?' said the sister encouragingly. 'You're her only visitor.'

'Of course.'

Turning at the door, she watched the nurse lead the old woman back to the ward. The frail bird-like head inclined towards the strong dark one. Watching, Alison knew exactly what she was going to do and why she had come.

The Dean's doctor was a man called Pearce, and the receptionist said he would be available in his office in ten minutes' time. She was so nervous that she could not bring herself to look directly at him. Subconsciously she expected him to look like the naval officer with the trace of a foreign accent who had spoken so ruthlessly to her on the troopship, and she was half afraid of what he might say to her. But when she sat down in the chair he placed for her and faced him across his desk, she saw that he was in no way like the officer. He was double-chinned and he wore a deaf-aid.

'Well, Mrs Osmond,' he began, 'perhaps you will tell me how I can help you?'

His voice numbed her. She did not know how or where to begin. Irrationally she found herself remembering the vicar who had prepared her for confirmation. He had insisted on her making her confession before receiving her first communion. She had been consumed with embarrassment partly because in the dim light of the incense-clouded church, she could not read the prayer of contrition from the faded card pinned to the prayer-desk, and partly because she could think of no sin suitable for the ears of her aunts' confessor. She remembered too the lecture he had given her because she had mentioned a name during the course of her confession. This had turned out to be the greatest of her sins in his eyes. She wondered why she should remember such a ridiculous episode at this moment.

Looking up, she was almost surprised to see that the doctor was wearing a white coat and stethoscope in place of a surplice and stole. He was a doctor, she told herself firmly, and not a priest. However puritanical his private opinions might be, it was not his place to condemn her morals.

'It's about the Dean – George Tindall,' she began nervously. 'I believe he's a patient of yours.'

'Yes?'

'I wondered how he was . . .' she tailed off, feeling ridiculous.

'I don't as a rule discuss my patients, unless of course you are a close relative?'

'No, of course not; I understand. I shouldn't have come.'

She stood up hastily, relieved at the prospect of escape.

'I suggest you say what you came to say, Mrs Osmond,' he said, not looking at her as he reached in his pocket for cigarettes.

'It isn't easy,' she began, clearing her throat.

'You have something to tell me concerning your relationship with Mr Tindall. Is that it?'

She remembered the old adage that women were supposed to fall in love with their priests and felt humiliated. How foolish she must seem to him.

He glanced at his watch. 'I suggest you tell me everything,' he said curtly, and so she did.

But she cheated in the telling. She exaggerated the Dean's feelings and played down her own. She did not tell him that at the time she had wanted the Dean at least as much as he had wanted her. She did not tell him that she had taken the initial step in their love-making. She did not tell him about the child she was now expecting nor of her guilt and unhappy feelings ever since its conception. She told him what she herself wanted to believe; that the affair had meant nothing to her either at the time or now, and that her reasons for coming at all were only to be of help to the Dean. She told him in the hope that he would wave a magic wand and tell her that all would now be well. Go home and sin no more.

It appeared that it did not make much difference what she said. He had drawn his own conclusions.

'So you are in love with your Dean,' he said mildly.

'Indeed I am not!' she cried, angrily denying what she did not want to admit.

'No?' He eyed her thoughtfully. 'Then why exactly are you here?'

'I'm certainly not in love with him,' she repeated hotly.

'It's not a criminal offence, you know. It's not particularly unique. In fact, a love affair at your age can be a very satisfying experience – if you will let it be.'

'I'm not in love with him,' she repeated, but she no longer convinced even herself.

He leaned towards her, his hands clasped on the table.

'Take an honest look at yourself, Mrs Osmond. At a guess I would say you are a woman with time on your hands. You are bored and comparatively young – ready for an emotional experience.'

'If you call having five children and running a large vicarage too little to do, try it,' she flung at him childishly.

He smiled. 'I apologise. I should have said comparatively little to do. It makes no difference to my argument.'

'Haven't you left out the Christian angle?' she asked defiantly, not ashamed to plug a code she no longer respected.

He scraped back his chair. 'You Christians make me smile. You take yourselves so seriously; you sin like everyone else but your consciences spoil it for you. Do you really know why you came to see me today? You wanted a confessor. Well, all right. I'm willing to take on that role if it will help you, but it's got to be an honest confession. Don't fool yourself into thinking you came here for Tindall's sake.'

She was silent, amazed at his perception and knowing that all he had said was true.

'I can't help you till you tell me the whole truth. Even a priest would tell you that, wouldn't he?'

She nodded. 'I feel ashamed.'

'You take yourself far too seriously.'

'Is that wrong?'

'It's extremely bad for you. Mental hygiene consists of laughing at yourself at least three times daily after meals. At a guess I would say you've found difficulty smiling once a week.' His eyes gleamed with sudden amusement. 'As a result you've made yourself miserable, not to mention your husband and family, and all because you refuse to admit that you have had a small affair of the heart. Other people have extra-marital relationships, but not you, Mrs Osmond. It's all right for them, but you are above that sort of thing. You try to tell me that you had intercourse because you were sorry for my patient. Do you really expect me to believe that? What's more important, can you really believe that yourself?'

She shook her head. 'Is it not possible then to have sex without the complications of love?' she asked.

'Of course it's possible, but it's rare with women like you. What interests me is that you should think sex without love the lesser sin. I should have thought that as a Christian you . . .'

'But I'm not a Christian,' she interrupted, eager now that he should know everything.

He laughed. 'Come, Mrs Osmond, try and be honest with yourself. You say you are not a Christian and yet you break one of the Christian laws and bring all this misery on yourself by way of punishment. You may find the practice of Christianity boring and the rules restricting, but you are a Christian, my friend. You are a typical Christian with a built-in guilt complex and an indecently enlarged conscience.'

He stood up, prepared to bring the interview to an end.

'I must go. I have another appointment at the other end of the hospital in five minutes' time,' he said, looking at his watch.

'But what about the Dean?' she asked.

'What about him?' he replied, crossing the room. 'I thought we had established that it was yourself you came to talk about.'

'It's not quite so simple.'

'I don't think you can serve any good purpose by seeing the Dean again. The affair, from his point of view, was, I should imagine, a symptom of his illness, not a cause. I don't think it all that important. In six months you will both have forgotten it happened.'

'That's impossible,' she said slowly, dropping her head. 'I'm going to have his child.'

'I see,' he replied slowly, closing the door he had just opened. 'Yes, I agree, that does rather complicate matters.'

'I don't think I can go through with it on my own. Someone must share the burden of knowing. I can't possibly tell my husband; it would destroy him. Who else can I tell?'

'Mm.' He thought for a moment. 'Ordinarily I would say go home and have your baby. You've shared the burden already by telling me. I think you could pull it off. Once the child was a person in his own right, you would concern yourself less and less with his conception. This is true of adopted parents. Your sense of duty would help you there. But I have my patient to consider too. I need some time to think this one out. Come back tomorrow or the next day when I've had time to sleep on it.'

'You've been a great help,' she said as he opened the door for her.

And it was true. As she left the hospital her heart was light. She felt as Christian must have done when he dropped his burden. She could now admit to herself what she knew to be the truth, that she loved the Dean, and yet strangely enough her love for Ken was not diminished. Rather, it too had increased. She realised that for two months now she had shut the door of her heart firmly in the face of all love and affection. In her subconscious refusal to recognise her true feelings, she had forced herself to withdraw not only from the love of her family, but from everyone else she had come in contact with. Now that she was able to open the door of her heart a crack, love rushed in, enriched and increased by her acknowledged love for the Dean. She knew now that there would be enough love for a sixth child, just as there had been love for the previous five. Her heart was an expanding organ. The more she loved, the more room there was for love. She did not think now that her love for the Dean had ever been predominantly sexual, any more than her love for Ken depended on habit and time. One could love two men at the same time.

But this was no new revelation. It had happened before in her life and the first time she had loved two men she had been ashamed and tried to hide it even from herself, just as she had tried to hide her love for the Dean.

It had happened some months after her affair with the fat boy had ended. She had fallen in love with a man ten years her senior. He was well-to-do, established in a good job and made no secret of the fact that he was looking for a wife. He was also shy, diffident and old-fashioned in his attitude towards her. She enjoyed going out with him. He had a car and would drive her out into the country where they would walk together under summer skies. They liked doing the same things and they soon became friends in the true sense of the word. It was weeks before he kissed her and when eventually he did, she did not at first feel the same desire for him as she had felt even for the fat boy. His undemonstrative manner towards her surprised her, for her other male friends were not so fastidious, but she liked his solicitous protective attitude and she admired his standards.

He bought her an engagement ring which she wore on a cord round her neck for she did not want to commit herself to a formal engagement. Basically she knew even then that she would never marry him. Nevertheless they continued to go out together and after a while their love-making reached a different stage.

It happened one hot afternoon in June. Up till that day their sex play had never extended beyond the limits of kissing uncomfortably in the car or lying on a waterproof-lined rug under spring-green beeches. They would lie for hours facing each other, their legs entwined and their lips touching. Sometimes he would slip his hand under her jersey and caress her back but no more.

On this particular afternoon, they were lying on the edge of a meadow fringed with buttercups. He opened his eyes briefly and saw a bee on her hair.

'There's a bee on you,' he said, flapping it away with his hand.

'Where?' she cried, twisting on to her back and suddenly he was lying on top of her and his kisses were hot as he rubbed his body softly and repeatedly against hers. After a while something frightening happened to her. It was like an electric shock that started deep inside her and spread throughout her body. It was beautiful, ecstatic and terrifying and she cried aloud. Flinging him off she sat up.

'What happened? What's wrong?' he asked anxiously.

'I don't know,' she said, but as she spoke she realised that she did know. She had had an orgasm. She lay back and looked up at his anxious face reddened by sun and sex.

'It's all right,' she said, smiling. 'It's really all right.'

'Marry me soon,' he said tensely.

'Perhaps I will,' she replied, and if she had not met Ken a few weeks later she might well have done, but she had known that Ken would be her husband long before he proposed to her and she had fallen in love with him even though his body was not yet as important to her as Gerald's.

So for a while she was in love with both men. She wanted to sleep with Gerald and she wanted to marry Ken. Of course it was Ken who won. She told Gerald about him one night as they were sitting in his car after a visit to the cinema. He took it badly. To comfort him and herself, for his distress was painful to her, she offered to go to bed with him, but he flung her offer aside.

'You want me to make a whore of you when I want to make you my wife.'

Dimly she knew that the time would come when she would have to choose between the Dean and Ken, just as she had had to choose between Gerald and Ken, but not yet. For the moment she loved them both and took pleasure in the expanding quality of her heart.

16

She returned to the empty vicarage in a state of cautious happiness. The whole world had taken on a brighter aspect coloured by the extent of her love. The quiet shabby house seemed kindlier, warmer, welcoming. Looking at herself in the hall-mirror, she was appalled by the dinginess of her appearance. The first thing to do when she had had something to eat was to wash her hair. As she stooped to pick up the afternoon post which was lying in a scatter on the floor, she had a sudden image of the Dean's hand lying loose in his lap as she had seen it through the glass partition that afternoon. She remembered how he had touched and caressed her and she trembled. How absurd she was being, she thought, but she did not care. She was old enough to know that happiness is momentary and for this moment she was grateful.

There was a postcard for her among the usual circulars and bills. She did not recognise the writing, but the signature leapt up at her from the paper. It was from Joan Tindall. Guilt made her almost afraid to read the neatly written paragraph, but all it contained was a request that she should send her congregation's contributions for the Deanery Annual Bazaar as soon as possible, and a reminder that the sale was on the following Friday.

With a pang of remorse she remembered that Mrs Smiley had left a parcel of knitted baby clothes and cotton aprons some weeks previously, with a note asking her to deliver them to the Deanery as soon as was convenient. She had completely forgotten.

Her first instinct was of dismay. She could not face the woman whose husband she had slept with, but her curiosity was aroused. She wanted to see his home and his wife too in the light of all that had happened. Although, up till now, Joan was everything that irritated her most in her own sex, the Dean had married her. He had lived under the same roof with her for twenty-five years. Something must have worn off.

Her fingers shook as she dialled the Deanery number and her voice sounded uncertain in her own ears as she introduced herself.

'Tomorrow afternoon?' Joan's voice held the same degree of aggressive condescension that it always assumed where Alison was concerned. It did not seem possible that she could be so unchanged considering everything, and Alison had to remind herself that as far as Joan was concerned, nothing had happened to make any difference to their relationship.

'I'm most frightfully busy this week, but I suppose tomorrow is as good a day as any other.'

Alison heard her leafing through her engagement book.

'Till tomorrow then,' Alison replied, more diffidently than she would normally have spoken, and rang off.

The following afternoon was perfect from the weather point of view. Already there were signs of spring in the greening under the twiggy hedges. The sea reflected the hills, mound for mound, and the sun was almost hot through the windscreen. In her nervousness Alison drove fast without noticing the scenery. She was already beginning to wish she had posted the goods for the bazaar.

Joan greeted her in a manner that managed to be both effusive and condescending at the same time. She was dressed in a well-made wool suit of indeterminate pastel tweed and her hair looked, as it always did, as if she had just come out of the hairdresser's.

'You'll stay for tea, of course,' she said, leading the way into the drawing-room, and Alison did not refuse as she would most certainly have done on former occasions. Her curiosity alone was enough to keep her; also she sensed in the older woman a need for companionship.

'Do sit down. I won't be many minutes.'

Joan handed her a glossy magazine and plumped a cushion on one of the arm-chairs before leaving the room, but Alison did not sit down. She gazed round the tidy room shaded by venetian blinds half-drawn to defy the spring sun. She tried to find something of the Dean in the furnishings, the reproductions of rose paintings, the china figurines and the deceptively simple flower arrangements, but she could find no trace of him. It occurred to her that he probably only came into this room when they had visitors. This room was Joan's reserved for bridge parties and callers like herself.

Stealthily she opened the door and looked out into the hall. Edge-to-edge pastel green carpeting, central heating radiators, a silver salver on the hall table, but again no sign of the Dean, nothing to indicate that he had so much as passed through. She opened another door, too curious now to care if she were discovered, and found herself in the dining-room. It smelled faintly of lavender polish and greens, and the table was covered with a crochet-trimmed cloth. She tried to picture him here, but with no success.

The next room was his study. As soon as she opened the door, she realised that the Dean was not a man to leave his mark on places. The study was as tidy and impersonal as an executive's office on television. Filing cabinet, book-case tidily stacked with theological volumes, with a shelf given over to mountaineering books, roll-top desk, all were spotless and orderly. Apart from the simple cross on the wall and a photograph of a group of deacons with a bishop, there was nothing to show that this room was different from any other office. She knew now that Joan was not responsible for this tidiness. This was very much his room and his way of living. That it was also Joan's was fortunate for them both. In this way at least they suited each other, and it was an important way. She had known a couple driven to divorce by the husband's perfectionist demands and his wife's slovenly house-keeping. The Dean would not be at home in Alison's untidy vicarage. Those attic rooms would drive him to despair. At the same time, she felt a stab of pity for them both. It seemed to her that the ability to leave personal belongings spread about the house, to stamp one's home with marks of identity, was a sign of security and happiness. Conversely the ultra-tidy home, the showroom house, revealed an insecure, possibly unhappy existence. It was as if the Dean had long ago learned not to give away too much of himself. He was as closed up as his own desk drawers. Without having to see it, she knew that Joan's kitchen would be the same.

'Did you want something?'

She turned to see Joan standing behind her with the tea tray.

'I was looking for the bathroom,' she replied brazenly.

Joan pointed to the cloakroom by the front door. The wash-basin with a clean towel hanging beside it could be seen clearly from where they stood.

'How stupid of me,' she replied.

It was not, however, in her nature to spy, and when she had closed the door behind her she dipped the edge of the towel into cold water to cool her flaming cheeks.

All his coats were here, neatly hung on hangers from the pegs. She crossed over and touched the black burberry he had worn that night. She pressed it to her face and smelled the cleaning fluids. There was a dry-cleaner's ticket pinned to the cuff. A sudden pang of yearning brought tears to her eyes and she turned away quickly and left the room.

Joan had set the tea on a small table covered with a hand-embroidered cloth. There were two sorts of home-made cake and paste sandwiches similar to those the Dean had had with him on the trip to Pendale.

'I hope you didn't go to all this trouble just for me,' Alison said politely.

Joan drew back her thin shoulders reprovingly. 'I always keep a plentiful supply of home-baking. We have so many callers.'

Instinctively Alison knew this was not true. Apart from the monthly bridge four and various official or congregational callers for the Dean, there would be few visitors in the week. This was not the sort of house one popped into, and yet Alison knew that poppers-in would be made welcome. She was very much aware of the loneliness of this sensitive, unrelaxed woman.

'I can never keep anything for more than a day,' she said, accepting a cake but refusing the sandwiches.

'I don't wonder at that! You have such a large family. I expect they eat you out of house and home. I'm sure I don't know how you cope.'

Joan was on easier ground for she tended to feel superior to fertile women. Alison remembered how the Dean had told her his wife had been relieved rather than disappointed when told he could not give her a child.

'I don't – cope that is,' Alison said with a faint smile.

'How you must relish the peace and quiet when they are all at school.'

Behind the trivial conversation, Alison could sense the anomaly of Joan's feelings. On the one hand, there was the relief of not having had to undergo childbirth and the responsibility of children, but there was also the envy of a lonely woman for the companionship of a family, the continual wondering at what had been missed.

'Not for long, however. I'm having another.'

She had not intended to say it, and yet, going over the conversation in her mind afterwards, she wondered if this had not been the main purpose of her visit. It gave her the excuse she needed to tell the Dean herself. It would not be fair for him to hear of her pregnancy from his wife.

'Oh really?' Joan said distantly. A faint flush tinged her cheek.

'Are you surprised?' Alison pressed her.

'A little perhaps . . .' The patches grew brighter. 'After all, in this day and age, with the world population being as it is . . .' she tailed off, not wishing to be openly rude.

Alison smiled. 'I hardly think one extra . . .'

'Ah, but if everyone were to say that, Mrs Osmond . . .'

Alison laughed. 'You ought to get a job in a birth control clinic,' she said unthinkingly. She could visualise Joan's wagging forefinger admonishing fecund wives, but she had not meant to be cruel.

'I don't find that remark amusing.'

Joan was hurt and shocked. It was a measure of their incompatibility that Alison was capable of making such a remark, even as a joke – particularly as a joke – to such a woman.

'I'm sorry,' she said contritely. 'I have an odd sense of humour.'

Her apology was accepted.

'I hope you don't speak to your husband's parishioners like that,' Joan said, literally wagging her finger this time.

'All the time, I'm afraid,' she replied lightly. 'No wonder they disapprove of me.'

It was a small lie which she told fully conscious of what she was doing. She wanted to restore Joan's feeling of superiority before bringing up the subject closest to her heart. It worked better than she could have hoped. Joan was smiling smugly secure in the knowledge that she knew how to behave.

'I'm sure they don't disapprove of you as much as you think, my dear. After all, with your family you have a great deal to contend with, as everyone knows.'

'How is the Dean?' Alison asked after a pause during which she accepted another cup of tea.

Joan's mouth tightened. The question had been asked so many times but she had not yet learned how to answer it.

'I'm expecting him home in a week or so, but of course, as I've told him repeatedly, and the doctor agrees, he'll have to do far less in the future. He never stops. Night after night, meetings and organisations, visiting, and the same in the afternoons. He's killing himself.'

Alison knew a number of clergy wives who found satisfaction in boasting of their husband's activities in the name of duty. In the Dean's case, she suspected it was true.

'Ken always says he works too hard,' she murmured.

'That trip to the city in January was the last straw.' She looked at Alison over her tea-cup. 'I've often wondered, how did he seem to you on that journey? He took you with him, didn't he?'

Alison had not expected that question and did not immediately know how to answer it.

'I can't think why you both attempted to come home on such a night,' she continued without a pause. 'It was sheer madness. Could you not have persuaded him to stay in Pendale another day?'

'He's a difficult man to persuade,' Alison said with a shade of a smile, 'but you must know that.'

'Difficult?' she echoed sharply. 'I have never found him difficult. Dedicated perhaps, but not difficult.'

She was on the defensive at once, a woman who knew only too well her husband's obstinacies.

'Do you think it was the journey that was responsible for his being in hospital now?'

'As I said, it was the last straw. He caught a severe chill which certainly added to his depression.' She turned on Alison accusingly. 'How did he get so wet? His coat was soaking and his shoes too. I'm surprised he didn't get pneumonia.'

The shepherd's wife had dried his clothes thoroughly before they left the cottage. He must have gone somewhere else after leaving her in the hotel, but Joan was waiting for an answer.

'He did a lot of digging. We were stuck in a drift,' she replied uneasily.

'I see.'

Joan looked down at her carefully manicured nails as if trying to make up her mind. Then she looked up and Alison realised that she wanted to talk but did not know where to start. She had probably not spoken with honesty to any other person; with Alison it was possible because subconsciously she believed Alison's pregnancy and large family more of a disaster than her own sick husband. With her bridge friends and members of the congregation, she would feel compelled to belittle the Dean's illness. There were still plenty of people who considered a spell in a mental hospital as a disgrace.

'He didn't speak at all, not for days. I tried to get out of him what was wrong, but it was as though I no longer existed. And then I found out that he was arriving late for services. I took to driving him right to the vestry door, but he would dither. George dither! The organist would have to come out and talk him inside . . .' she broke off, 'but I expect you've heard all about it. People talk.'

'I haven't heard. All Ken told me was that the Dean was in hospital. He isn't particularly communicative where his fellow clergy are concerned.'

'Isn't he?' Joan looked up in sudden understanding. 'I suppose most of the clergy are the same. That last Sunday George was standing in the pulpit just as he does every Sunday, but the words would not come. He just stood there. In the end the organist had to go and bring him down. It was he who told me I ought to call the doctor, that George had not been himself for some time. But of course I knew that.'

Alison's hand tightened on her cup as she thought of the Dean inarticulate.

'But he's better now?'

'Yes, I suppose so, oh, I don't know. The doctors say very little and George himself – he's like your husband – is uncommunicative. They all say he needs a long rest, but he isn't that sort of person. He can't rest. If he isn't working, he's walking and then he gets overtired. To tell you the truth, I sometimes wonder if he'll ever get really well again. Sometimes I think . . .'

She broke off, aware that she was on the verge of saying more than she had previously allowed herself to consider.

'What do you think?' Alison urged, wondering if she had guessed something of what had happened in the cottage.

'It's ridiculous, really, but there are times when I get the impression that he doesn't want to get better.'

'Why should you say that?' she asked softly, careful to hide her overwhelming curiosity.

'It's something I can't put into words, but I sometimes think he's afraid to – to let himself feel. I wish I could explain better. He doesn't laugh, he doesn't get angry. Nothing shocks him or pleases him. It's as if something inside him has died. He used to be such an enthusiastic sort of person. I was always the dull one.' She laughed nervously. 'Does that sound strange to you?'

Alison shook her head, astounded that this seemingly imperceptive woman could have got so close to the truth.

'Perhaps he's forgotten how to live – perhaps we both have.' Joan sighed and added with a return to her old manner, 'I can't think why I'm boring you with all this. You can't possibly be interested in all our troubles. Do have some more tea.'

The telephone rang and Joan rose immediately to answer it. Alison could hear her high irritating voice talking and talking. She looked round the room again. How had he endured all those years? she wondered. How had Joan? Perhaps it was best that they had lost the ability to feel anger and love, pity and hate. Perhaps in their silent separate farce of a marriage they had achieved a certain contentment.

No one, she thought, could see into another marriage, yet theirs was so little of a marriage that she suspected there was nothing much to see. Their lives unfurled themselves before her as simply as a leaf in spring. Joan would rise and make breakfast. The Dean would rise and pray. They would meet briefly for a meal at which they would look at their letters and he would glance at the paper. He would go into his study and she to her polishing and baking. They would meet again for lunch during which they would listen to the radio news, and after which he would go out visiting and she out to the shops. They would meet again briefly for supper before the evening round of meetings, choir practice or similar activities. She too would be fully occupied in the evenings with Mothers' Union, Guilds and bridge. They would meet again to do the evening chores, tend the fires, lock up. She would potter, tidying cushions, washing up stray cups and ash-trays, folding newspapers. He would go into his study and do what? Her imagination lingered on that intimate hour. Joan would be in bed long before he came upstairs. She would not even hear him for the door between their rooms was closed.

It was no marriage and yet was it so very different from countless other marriages? Was it so very different from her own? She was appalled to realise that, apart from a few minor differences, she might have been describing her own life with Ken. Obviously the children made a difference and so did sex, but not as much difference as all that. If Joan and the Dean lived in a web of silence, so did she and Ken.

She shifted uneasily in her chair, disliking the direction of her thoughts. Joan finished her telephone conversation and came back with a formal smile.

'I'm sorry about that,' she said with a return to her old brisk manner. 'The telephone simply never stops. I expect it's the same with you.'

'My eldest son says that it's a sign of maturity if you can let it ring,' Alison said, standing up and preparing to go.

It was meant to be a light remark, but Joan took it seriously.

'Oh, I don't think that's at all a good idea. Supposing it was something important for your husband. A vicar is so like a doctor in that respect . . .'

'They can always ring again,' Alison replied lightly, 'and now I really must go.'

On the way home, Alison made up her mind. If the Dean's inability to feel had landed him in a mental home, she had the power to awaken him. She had done it before and she could do it again. Whether or not the doctor approved, she would use that power. Certainly she wanted to go to him and tell him that she loved him for her own sake, but also for the Dean's sake and even for Joan's, or so she told herself. She believed that the woman loved her husband in her own way and wanted to see him happy. She, Alison, had the ability to send him back to his wife able to feel compassion and understanding for her, if not desire and devotion. But as she continued the journey back to the vicarage, she knew that once again she was not being honest with herself. All those high-flown ideals were no more than excuses – pitifully transparent even to herself. She did not care tuppence for Joan's feelings, nor for her marriage. She was in love and to hell with everyone else. That was the real truth.

17

She faced Dr Pearce with more composure than she felt.

'I've made up my mind. I'm going to tell him. It's my clear duty.'

A note of defiance had already crept into her voice as if she expected him to forbid her.

'Duty, Mrs Osmond?' He looked at her quizzically.

'I'm sure I can help him.'

'So you intend to tell him regardless of what I may advise, out of a sense of duty?' He sounded amused.

'I do.'

'Somewhat of a paradox, don't you think?'

'I don't understand.'

'I think you do, Mrs Osmond.'

'You think I should say nothing,' she stated flatly.

'On the contrary. In this particular case I happen to agree with you. A jolt such as you propose to give Tindall should be at least as effective as half a dozen more conventional treatments. Just one thing, however . . .'

She looked up expectantly.

'Don't bring duty into it. This has nothing to do with duty. If you want to sleep with my patient again . . .'

'No,' she interrupted quickly.

He held up his hand. 'If you want to sleep with my patient again, good luck to you. If you can lift his depression by raising his blood pressure, I have no objection, but don't strangle your intention by tying it up with fancy motives and a sense of duty.'

She flushed. 'There's more to it than that,' she began. For the moment she hated him for his clear sight and herself for her transparency.

'There always is,' he told her and opened the door of his office. 'It's a fine afternoon. Get him to go out, if you can. To my knowledge he hasn't stirred from the ward since he arrived. We have some fine grounds round the hospital.'

'You've spoiled it all,' she said petulantly.

'Nonsense,' he told her, 'but if it will make you feel any better, I prescribe the treatment. A satisfactory love affair is as good a therapy as I know.'

She knew he was laughing at her, but she also knew she had his blessing, and because she was by nature obedient, this was more important to her than she would have cared to admit.

He was sitting in the same window where she had seen him before, dressed in a soft collar and reading. This time, however, he was alone. The sight of him filled her with such nervousness that if a passing nurse had not stood back holding the door open for her to go in she might never have found the courage.

No one paid her any attention as she crossed the room. In this particular ward visitors came and went as they pleased, indistinguishable from the patients. She stood looking down on him and noticed that his hair had a long un-healthy sick-room appearance.

'Hullo, George,' she said quietly.

He looked up at the sound of her voice, his face expressionless. For a moment she thought he was not going to speak to her, and then she remembered that his depression had taken the form of silence. When eventually he spoke, his voice was harsher and more authoritative than she remembered.

'What are you doing here?'

She had forgotten he could sound so rude.

'I came to see you,' she said uncertainly.

'I don't think that we have anything to say to each other.'

She had a moment of panic. Dr Pearce had warned her that his original declaration of love may well have been a symptom of his troubled mind and not a cause. It looked as if he were cured. Obviously he no longer cared for her. Perhaps he had forgotten the whole episode. Perhaps, she thought in a wild moment of panic, she had dreamed the whole affair. The man who faced her now seemed in no way to be connected with the man she had held in her arms.

'You may have nothing to say to me, but I have something of importance to tell you,' she continued, forcing herself to be calm.

'Then I suggest you say it.'

'We can't talk here. Let's go outside and walk a bit.'

He rose reluctantly, but hesitated only a moment before leading the way through a side door which opened into a formal garden bright with forget-me-nots and wallflowers. A number of patients were strolling across the sunlit lawn or sitting on garden seats sheltered by hedges and shrubs. Beyond the garden the ground sloped towards a shallow stream, the banks of which were lined with tall smooth beeches. Wood anemones bordered the informal paths that meandered between the trees and beside the stream. It would be cool and lush in summer, but it was warm and beautiful under the pale March sun.

They came to a wooden bridge that spanned the stream, and stood looking down at the water. Although he seemed older, more distant, different, every cell in her body was aware of him.

'There's a fish under that stone,' she said to break the silence between them.

'Is that what you came to say?' he asked coldly.

'No, of course not.'

She looked down at his hands, familiar, thick-veined, on the railing of the bridge and longed to cover them with her own, but she did not dare. The gulf between the lover of her memory and the man beside her widened with every second.

'I came to say how sorry I am . . .'

'Sorry? Why?' he interrupted.

'You must know why.' It was not what she had meant to say, but she was finding it increasingly difficult to say anything.

'I don't require your pity,' he said shortly, deliberately misunderstanding. 'Mental breakdowns are occupational hazards of the clergy, but I'm sure you must know that.' He shifted impatiently on the bridge and looked at his watch. 'Now that you've said what you no doubt felt you ought to say, I suggest you go home. There can be little point in prolonging this conversation.'

He turned and began to walk away across the bridge and along a path that led through a wilder tangle of decayed winter undergrowth. It was almost as if he were afraid to listen to more.

'That isn't what I came to say – at least not altogether,' she said, following him as best she could. 'Please listen to me.'

'I can't stop you talking.'

He was still walking but more slowly now.

'Then please wait a minute. I can't keep up with you.'

He paused and half-turned. The massive trunk of a beech tree spread across the track they were following and she leaned against it and tried to control her breathing. A blackbird was singing its head off in a branch above them. Its piercing cheerfulness sounded incongruous in her ears. The Dean plucked a tight brown beech bud and rolled it between his fingers.

'Well?' he said at length, still not looking at her. The sun gleamed on his glasses as he moved his head in a well-remembered gesture.

'I have to tell you how it is with me.'

She rubbed the palms of her hands against the pewter-smooth trunk behind her back.

'Well?' he repeated, his voice only a little less cold.

She began by telling him how unhappy she had been for the past two months; how her attitude to life had changed and how she had withdrawn from her friends and been moody and difficult with Ken.

He listened in silence with his head sunk on his chest and his forefinger crooked against his lower lip. She remembered, irrelevantly, that it was the way he sat in church to listen to the choir's anthem.

'Then I made a discovery,' she continued hesitatingly, 'at least, to be honest, it was Dr Pearce who . . .'

'Dr Pearce?' he repeated, frowning.

'Please let me tell it my own way. Dr Pearce was very helpful. He pointed out why I had been so difficult, confused . . .'

She paused. Whichever way she might use to lead up to it, the truth was hard to say and he gave her no help.

'He told me that I was deliberately keeping the truth from myself and as soon as he explained, I knew he was right.'

'I don't understand,' he said at length.

'I'm in love with you.'

The words had been said and having said them once she wanted to go on saying them.

'I've been in love with you all the time, but I refused to face it because I was afraid and ashamed.' She turned her head away. 'I'm not afraid any more.'

He was silent for so long that eventually she turned to look up at him. He was staring at the thick root of the tree which erupted out of the path.

'Have you nothing to say to me?' she asked uncertainly.

He stirred. 'Why are you telling me all this now?'

'I had to say that I was sorry. I hurt you that morning. When I look back and remember some of the things I said, I am so ashamed. It was simply that I was so afraid that I had to lie.'

'You were right to be afraid.'

'No,' she said with returning confidence. 'Fear solves nothing. I know that now.'

'And what of me?' he asked abruptly.

'I don't understand . . .' she began.

More and more she had the feeling that she was talking to a stranger. This was not the man she remembered, still less the lover, and yet this flesh and blood reality was even more desirable to her than the creature of her memory.

He looked at her for the first time and there was no warmth in his eyes.

'You are so involved in your own feelings that you seem to have forgotten mine. Did it never occur to you that I too might be afraid?'

She was speechless.

'You say you care, but let me ask you this. If you had given one thought to me, would you have come here today?

I don't think so. You would have tried to put the whole matter out of your mind. Once you told me that the love you talk about so glibly was an impossibility, and you were right. Did it not once occur to you that I might want to forget an episode that can only be sordid and shameful in retrospect? In time I might even have succeeded. Why did you have to come back?'

Behind the harsh words, she sensed his anguish and knew that he had been no more successful than she in forgetting. She went close to him and touched him briefly.

'It's better that there should at least be truth between us. Surely it's better to recognise our feelings for what they are and admit them – at least to each other and ourselves – than to refuse to admit they exist. That way lies madness. I know, for if you have been out of your mind with depression lately, then, believe me, so have I.'

'How can there ever be truth between us? Such a fruit of the spirit can never grow from a corrupt root.'

'Can love ever be corrupt?' she asked softly. 'Oh yes, I agree, lust and sex are probably not on for people like us, but if by admitting that I love you, I can be a nicer person, easier to live with, more gentle at home, then how can it be wrong? If you can leave this place and go back to your wife able to talk to her because there is love in your heart for me, then surely ours must be a good love?'

He shook his head slowly.

'We're not teenagers searching for mates,' she continued. 'The jealousies and demands of young lovers have nothing to do with us. Our love could be a good thing, good for us and good for those most concerned with us. The more I love you, the more love I have for others. This can't be wrong. I wish I could make you understand for I feel so strongly about it that I'm sure I'm right.'

He turned then, and for the first time he looked directly at her. 'Alison, Alison,' he said sadly, 'you are like all your sex. Don't you know by this time that feelings are the blindest of guides?'

'Not in this case . . .'

'In every case. You plead well, and perhaps it could be all as you say in a rosy cosy world with no sin.'

'It could be like that with us. I know it could.'

He shook his head. 'Perhaps your heart is big enough, though I doubt it. No human heart is big enough, certainly not mine.'

'All we have to do is love each other. You make it seem a Herculean task.'

'And you make it sound too easy. Love is difficult. It requires skill and hard work and infinite patience. It needs complete selflessness and an enormous amount of energy. I'm too old for that sort of love; too old and tired and numb to care. Can you understand that?' He looked down at her eager face. 'No, probably not. You are younger than me and you have been surrounded with love all your life. Love comes easily to you, therefore you are able to give it easily. I stopped wanting love long before we met. Human love means very little to me. That night we got caught in the blizzard I made some sort of attempt to recapture what might have been. But it was a moment of sheer madness. My only excuse is that when it happened I was not entirely in my right mind. When you told me the next day how you felt I was sick with self-disgust and shame, but I was not broken-hearted. Perhaps my pride was a little damaged, but I was none the worse for that.'

'Then why are you here?' she asked simply.

He appeared not to have heard her for he continued as if she had not spoken.

'When I said to you that it was all best forgotten I was right. Even if we were free to love each other, I don't think it would work. As it is, we are not free, as you were the first to point out on the last occasion we met, and all your beautiful theories can't make a virtue out of what is basically a sin. You must know that.'

'I don't know it,' she insisted. 'I don't believe that love between us could be a sin. Lord, how I hate that word!' she added impatiently. 'I don't believe there is any such thing as sin. It's just a synonym for pleasure conjured up by pulpit-bashers and confessors.'

He sighed and made a small gesture towards her with his hand.

'Man is a moral animal. Without his code of right and wrong he disintegrates. And now you must go home. You should never have come.'

'But you're glad I came, nevertheless,' she said quietly, knowing it to be true.

'You and I have nothing more to say to each other,' he said sadly.

She knew she should have turned her back on him then as he was trying so hard to do to her. All he had said had cost him an effort. He looked tired. It was her turn to make the next effort. She recognised that they had reached a turning point in their relationship. She should have ended it there, but she could not do it.

'We have, George; oh God, we have!'

He looked up, quick to sense the change in her tone.

'I'm pregnant.'

'I don't understand.' He frowned. 'How does this concern me?'

'I think the baby is yours.'

'Mine! But that's impossible. I told you,' he said quickly.

'You told me your wife had never conceived and you told me you had mumps when you were a child. It was natural to jump to certain conclusions, but people can live together for years and not have children. It doesn't necessarily mean . . .'

'I know that,' he interrupted sharply.

'Did you have any tests?'

'It didn't seem necessary.' He looked at her closely. 'Are you certain?'

'About the child? Yes, I'm certain.'

'That's not what I meant.'

'It's yours,' she said quietly.

'Merciful God, what can I say?'

He turned from her in real distress, but she went close to him and put her hand on his arm.

'I'm happy to have your child.'

'Does Kenneth know?' he asked presently.

'About the child? Of course.'

'But not . . . ?'

'No.'

'When will you tell him?'

'I won't tell him, and nor will you.'

'But it's my child – my child!' he exclaimed, turning to her and putting his hands on her shoulders, almost shaking her. She had not bargained for such a reaction.

'You will know it and so will I, but no one else.'

'Oh God, it's too much to ask.'

'What else can we do?' she pleaded. 'Perhaps I shouldn't have told you. It was unfair of me.'

'Shouldn't have told me? What are you talking about?' he cried. 'It's my child. I have the right to know.' He paused and added in a different tone, 'If you knew how much I want a son.'

She moved close to him and put her head against his shoulder.

'I know,' she said.

His body was tense and she could hear the beat of his heart.

'Be still,' she said, embracing him. Her arms felt heavy with tenderness. She wanted to cradle him, hold him close almost as if he were the child within her.

'I must have time to think,' he said, moving away from her.

'Of course. I'll go now.' She turned to leave him.

'You're good at that, aren't you?'

The change in his voice stopped her dead and when she turned she saw that he was blazing with anger.

'You make me fall for you like a besotted schoolboy and leave me to face the consequences. Now you tell me you are going to have my child and there's not a thing you intend to do about it. What sort of a woman are you?'

She was speechless, amazed at the force of his anger, the anger of a life-time of suppression.

Then she said, 'I deserved that. I'm sorry.'

'It's not enough,' he said, his voice still clipped with anger. 'It's not enough to be sorry. Don't you see that?'

'What do you want me to do?'

'For God's sake how should I know? I don't understand you, how your mind works, anything about you.'

'How could you? I don't understand myself.'

His anger ceased as suddenly as it had risen.

'Forgive me,' he said, reaching out for her hand. 'I had no right to speak to you like that.'

'I love you,' she said, drawing close to him.

They embraced with tenderness, standing together without speaking, at peace with each other until they heard footsteps close to them in the dry leaves. An idiot lad with Mongol eyes was staring at them. He pointed and gestured incomprehensibly, but the Dean, it seemed, knew and understood him.

'Danny has come to tell me it's tea-time,' he said gently. 'He won't go away without me.'

She moved away from him. 'I'll come back,' she told him. 'I promise.'

There was a short cut to the main gates. She turned once to look back at him. The boy had put his hand in his and they were walking back across the sunlit lawn. It occurred to her that leaving him then was one of the hardest things she had ever had to do in her life. She knew now that her bright easy theories about love were fantasies woven by her self-deceiving imagination.

18

The bazaar was in full swing. Townswomen with empty shopping bags crowded into the church hall intent on the cake stall. A tall man with a lugubrious expression that hid a sharp sense of humour teased the women into parting with silver instead of pence at the door. Alison knew him slightly.

'What a good turn-out,' she remarked as she paid for her tea ticket.

'Of people possibly; of pockets, that remains to be seen.'

She laughed and someone turned with a glare and told her to be quiet. Inside, the Dean's wife, as convener, was introducing the opener, some minor member of the aristocracy with a history of generosity to the Church.

While the speaker was making the conventional exhortations to spend, Alison looked round the hall. It was packed, and the plentiful stalls showed how much organisation had gone into making the afternoon successful. Alison, who knew from personal experience just how much work was entailed in organising this sort of affair, was impressed. Never good herself at convening similar fund-raising events, she was glad that Joan should have her hour of triumph.

Polite clapping indicated that the speech was over and Joan brought the opener down from the platform to take her round the stalls. Alison caught Joan's eye over the bent bobbing hats round the work stall, and smiled. Joan returned the greeting perfunctorily and turned away to talk in a loud proprietary manner – or so it seemed to Alison – about the Dean to some acquaintance who, like everyone else present, would, during the course of the afternoon, find time to ask.

'He's very much better, thank you,' Alison heard her say with a complacent smile. 'Oh yes, entirely caused by overwork . . . I'm expecting him any day now.'

She turned to someone else and repeated almost word for word what she had just said. Filled with a sudden unreasonable jealousy, Alison could bear no more. She turned and left the hall without having bought anything. The lugubrious door-keeper thought she had been overcome by the crowd and heat and she let him believe it. She took her car out of the car-park and drove straight to the hospital.

She saw him ahead of her, walking up the hospital drive, and she stopped the car. He seemed as surprised to see her there as she was to see him, but he was not, as she was, disconcerted. Although it was only two days since she had seen him he seemed different. There was an air of calmness about him that she had never known him to possess. He was like a man who had reached a decision.

'I'm afraid I cut the sale,' she said, winding down the window to speak to him, not hiding her pleasure in his appearance.

'The sale? Dear me, I'd forgotten about the sale.'

'Come for a drive,' she suggested impulsively.

He hesitated for a moment and seemed to make up his mind.

'I'll have to let them know.'

While she waited she looked at her reflection in the driving mirror. For the first time in her life she wished she were younger and beautiful. She hated the lines at the corners of her eyes and the faint rings round her neck. She looked at her hair closely. There was no white to be seen, but it seemed to have lost some of its lustre. She wondered if the time had come to start on coloured rinses. Thus she kept her mind occupied with trivial thoughts to control her excited anticipation.

'Where would you like to go?' she asked, leaning across the front seat to open the door for him.

'To the sea, I think.'

Gardens were pink and gold with flowering currant and daffodils in the sunlight as they drove through the suburbs and out into the open country. Here the fields were beginning to show green and sheep browsed patiently as they awaited the birth of their lambs. She took a turning off the main road and soon the sea, mild and blue as speedwells, was spread before them. It was a place she very often used to come to with the boys, but she had no thought of them now as she stopped the car on the grass verge. They sat for a moment in silence looking at the view.

'Let's walk,' she suggested presently.

'Why not?' he agreed.

Apart from comments on the miraculous March weather, neither of them had said much on the drive, and now as they walked downhill towards the dunes, they did not speak at all, but it was a companionable silence. She became more and more aware of the change in him. It was almost as if he were happy, but she could not be sure. She had never known him happy.

The sharp sea-grass tore her stockings and scratched her legs and a sudden stiff breeze blew her hair across her face and ruffled the still water. It also brought the colour to his face and reminded her of their walk in the mountains. She wondered if he remembered too.

'Let's go to the rocks,' she said, pointing a short distance along the shore. 'It might be more sheltered.'

He strode across the shingle, enjoying the exercise, and she had to half run to keep up with him. Her shoes, unsuitable for the occasion, sank in the soft sand, and by the time they had reached the shelter of the rocks, she was out of breath.

'Let's sit for a while,' she said, finding a smooth rock and emptying the sand out of her shoes.

He sat down a few yards away from her and leaned back against the rock and closed his eyes. The sun beat down on them with surprising warmth. Apart from the quiet murmur of the sea, the silence was so great that she could hear a dog barking in a cottage on the main road.

'George,' she began after a few moments, 'we must talk.'

'No,' he said quietly, without opening his eyes. 'Don't say anything. It's not necessary.'

She looked across, longing to be nearer to him.

'What do you mean?'

'There's a letter for you in the mail. Strangely enough, I was posting it when you arrived. It says everything that must be said between us.' He paused and opened his eyes to look at her. 'I never thought we would meet again alone like this. This afternoon is time out of eternity, stolen perhaps, or perhaps freely given. Let us exist for an hour or so without asking questions, without complications, without past or future.'

'Future?' she repeated uncertainly. The finality of his words chilled her and she covered her face with her hands. He came over and sat on the rock beside her.

'No,' he said, drawing her hands from her face and putting an arm round her shoulders. 'Don't be unhappy.'

'How can I help it?'

'Remember – no past to give pain, no future to dread, only us now, together.'

'I love you,' she said, clasping his hand. His arm tightened on her shoulder, but for the moment he said nothing. They sat looking at the rise and fall of the water.

'Have you ever noticed,' he said, 'that the paler the sky is, the bluer the sea?'

He took his hand from hers and gently turned her face towards him.

'As blue as your eyes, Alison. The whole sea is in your eyes, the whole world.'

Under the intensity of his gaze, her eyes filled with tears. With a gentle forefinger he smoothed them from her cheeks.

'You're beautiful,' he said quietly.

She had been right to think him different. For the first time since she had known him, he was in complete charge of the situation. Today he would not shiver or weep or lose his temper.

'Oh, George, if only . . .'

His finger moved from her cheek and rested across her lips.

'Your hair is like sand with the sun on it.'

'Is there no way out?' she whispered.

His finger pressed more firmly on her lips. 'No past,' he said, 'no future.'

He was right, of course. There could be no sharing of this love. How naive, how foolish she had been to think for a minute that her heart that was now stretched to breaking point with love for George could contain even one other person. His hand moved from her face and lay across her stomach.

'Will he have hair like sand in the sun?' he asked.

'It might be dark and stiff like the bristles of a brush,' she replied with a gleam of a smile, and she touched his hand.

With a gesture that was at the same time sexless and yet

170

full of love, he opened the buttons of her jacket and slid his hand against her breast.

'Will you feed him yourself?' he asked.

Only to feel his hand there was enough to send the pain and anguished yearning shooting out from her womb. She covered his hand with her own and pressed it against her.

'I promise,' she said.

She knew he was not going to make love to her, but for the moment she did not care. They were closer now than sex could bring them. She reached up and took off his glasses.

'I want to see you properly,' she told him.

'Fine,' he said, smiling, 'so now I can't see you.'

Looking deep into his eyes, she saw deeper into his soul. All at once she was aware of his fears, his humiliations, his strivings and failings. Shaken with wonder and compassion for what she could see yet could never properly express, she said, 'You are a good man, George.'

'And you are lovely.'

She was aware that for human beings to see each other as wholly good and beautiful – if only for a few minutes – was in itself a small miracle.

He stood up and drew her into the circle of his arms. She could not feel the outline of his body through the material of his coat, but his lips trembled for an instant when they touched hers. When at last they moved apart, they walked towards the sea. Grey now, like his eyes, it nudged the shore too lazy to unfold a foamy wave. Looking down at their reflections, she saw two worlds, the real one of themselves against the sky and the wavering dream world where they lay together on wet sand and waving weed. She had a longing for the dream.

'If only life would end now,' she said, wondering what it would be like to die in his arms.

'Our life has ended,' he replied, and she knew it to be true.

Even if she were to plead and weep, she could not change his mind. She might succeed in breaking his heart, in destroying his peace, but she could not change his knowledge of what was right and what was for him – for them both – wrong. His life, his real life was with Joan in the quiet tidy house they shared. Hers was with Ken and her sons. Suddenly she remembered the child.

'You're wrong,' she said, 'our life has not yet properly started.'

A flurry of rain drove them back to the shelter of the overhanging cliffs. She shivered, and when he drew her to him for warmth, she opened the buttons of his coat and pressed against him. She wanted him as she had wanted him that night in the storm.

'I have so much tenderness to give you,' she said softly. 'I want to show you how much.'

She remembered the night in the cottage, how she had used him to satisfy her own needs. It occurred to her that if she were to be punished for her cruelty to him then, it would be this; never to have the chance to show him how much she really cared.

'If I take you now,' he said, his lips against her hair, 'we will never be able to leave each other again. Is that what you really want?'

'I don't know,' she said, 'truthfully I don't know.' But instinctively she moved away.

They walked back to the car slowly, their hands touching. Out of the shelter of the rocks, the wind rippled the water and turned the air cold. They sat in the car for a moment unwilling to end the afternoon. She felt again the stirring of desire, this time a last desperate attempt to remain with him a little longer. She turned to see an answering heat in his own eyes.

'George,' she put out her hand to him.

'Drive away,' he said, turning his head from her.

'Please,' she began.

'Drive away,' he repeated firmly.

She switched on the ignition and turned the car.

'Leave me where you found me at the main gates,' was all he said on the way back to the hospital.

The journey passed too quickly. Before he got out, he said to her, 'I'm going home tomorrow.'

'So soon!'

She could not help the note of desolation that had crept into her voice. Back in the tidy Deanery he would be lost to her forever.

'Sooner than expected certainly, but there was no point in staying here longer. There is nothing more they can do for me.'

'There is nothing anyone can do for you now, George. You're better. I've known it ever since I first saw you this afternoon, and I'm glad.'

He lifted her hand and kissed it gently.

'I love you,' she said at length.

'Goodbye, Alison,' he said, returning her hand to her lap.

'I love you,' she repeated, closing her eyes so that she did not have to see him go.

He opened the door and got out. When she heard it shut, she opened her eyes in a panic.

'George!' she called, but he did not turn. Through a mist of tears she watched his tall awkward figure move out of sight.

19

The letter in the unfamiliar handwriting was delivered the following morning. There was also a letter from her youngest son. She opened the latter and glanced quickly and almost irritably through the contents. There was no room in her heart for distractions of any sort.

... I was a sub in the Junior Team and we lost 11—0. It was a rotten match and a clumsy clot stood on my hand and mashed a finger. I got a tetanus jag. Could you send me 50 pence please because I've got some fines and also I've got to give 10 pence for a present for old Trout who's leaving (thank goodness). Only 14 days till the hols! Will you meet us at the station or come down and fetch us? We have to know because of journey money. ...

P.S. I've made a special calendar for you with 14 days to mark off till we're home!

She crushed the letter between her fingers. Only fourteen days; the holidays were almost here and in no way was she prepared for the onslaught of her sons. She hastily stuffed the crumpled letter into her pocket as if by putting it out of sight she could forget the contents, and picked up the other envelope.

The sight of it filled her with an active grief for she already knew what it must contain and could not bear the finality of it. A dozen times during the morning she picked it up and looked at it till the handwriting became as familiar to her as that on her son's. By the thickness of the envelope she knew it was a long letter and she trembled when she thought of the love she might read, if not openly, then between the lines.

The door-bell rang twice during the morning and the telephone seemed to be constantly ringing. She dealt with all the callers, whose business was for the main part with Ken, as quickly as common politeness would allow. Finally she took the letter out to the old summerhouse and opened the envelope.

The summerhouse was full of dust and cobwebs and the paraphernalia of a long-dead summer. She crouched down on a faded canvas stool and knew that she would be safe from intruders. Even Clem would not think to look for her here.

'Dear Alison,' she read. Her hand was shaking so much that she had to put the closely written sheets down on her knee.

'I have always found it easier to write rather than speak my thoughts, so that is why I have chosen this way to reply to what you so bravely came to tell me face to face. Perhaps I am being (yet again) a coward. In times past I have considered my reluctance to be drawn into emotional situations as a sign of strength but now I am not so sure. I ask only that you forgive me if, unwittingly, I have hurt you by writing rather than seeking a further interview.'

She smiled faintly at the stilted opening, but could not help wondering if she would have felt so indulgent if she had not already had that 'further interview'.

'I have given much thought to our conversation,' she read

on, 'and indeed for the past two days I have thought of little else. After much deliberation I came to the only conclusion possible under the circumstances. I believe that you will find yourself in agreement with me once you have learned my reasons and understood my motives.'

She sighed a little, wondering if even he could convince her against the whole force of her emotions.

'When you told me that your feelings for me enriched your experience of love to such an extent that you were able to give more to your family and friends, I knew that your love must be innocent in a way that mine could never be. If I were to let mine grow unhindered there would be room only in my heart for the beloved. I have already so little to give to my fellow-men I dare not give them less. Do you understand?'

Yes, she thought sadly, I understand.

'Then again,' she read on, 'I have looked back carefully over the long years of my marriage, dull perhaps, actively unhappy at times, but with rare moments of content; not totally wasted years until I start comparing them with what might have been, what might yet be if we were willing to risk the happiness of those who have done nothing to deserve such treatment from us. Neither of us could base our personal happiness on the misery of others. There would be no real happiness for you apart from your family, but you don't need me to tell you that.'

She knew it with her head though she could not yet grasp it with her heart. She had not thought so far or so deeply as this. She had not dared.

'It crossed my mind that we could perhaps meet occasionally to talk or be still together just to enjoy the comfort of each other's company, but this too I rejected. It would never work, for love between a man and a woman cannot stand still. We cannot arrange to meet – say on Thursdays – as ordinary friends may do, because my wife is at the guild and your husband at choir practice. We cannot pigeonhole our lives into tight little boxes. What happens on Thursday affects how we behave on Fridays, perhaps a month or a year later. What happened on one such Thursday has altered our lives and brought a third into being. It is an awesome thought.

'And now that I have mentioned the child, I must write more fully on that which belongs to you and me in a particularly wonderful and personal way. This I find hardest of all to do. I would like to claim my son and you as his mother and love and cherish you both. You, however, prefer to say nothing and this I can understand, although I am not convinced that Kenneth and Joan should be kept in ignorance of all that has happened. Do we, perhaps, underestimate – insult even – their capacity for understanding and forgiveness? I feel that our motives are not entirely honest, that we are keeping silent because silence is the easy way out. Be that as it may, I will keep silent if that is what you want. Should you, however, change your mind and decide to tell your husband, you have my whole-hearted consent and approval.'

Oh, George, she thought, I don't care how much I insult Ken's intelligence as long as I don't damage his heart.

'Dearest Alison,' – her heart lurched at the endearment – 'do I seem full of pious speeches and preaching morality? I do not want you to think that I regret what has happened between us. You were right when you said that love can be a good and enriching experience. Only its misuse is wrong and that is what I chiefly fear, for the misuse of love is, like a serpent in the soul, able to poison the whole personality. That is why there must be no further communication between us. That is why the affair must end before it is properly started.

'Don't misunderstand me. I am not suggesting we stop loving each other. How could I stop loving you when you have taught me the meaning of love? This illness of mine – I do not propose to dwell on it – is over because of you. Where I was blind, I can now see and where I was once dead, I am alive, and for my life, my dearest, I have you to thank. But we have to stop meeting and we have to stop dreaming. Does this sound hard? It is hard but there is, for us, no other way.

'I'm leaving Lethey Bridge in a day or two. There is no reason to stay for I am well again and ready for work. If the next few days are hard for you, remember how they will be for me.

'I have never found it easy to speak of God in a personal way, but this much I can say. What we feel for each other can be shared with Him. This promise I make to you. No day shall pass without my laying you and what is yours and mine together, before Him.

'Beloved, I don't want to stop writing to you for this must be the last letter. God bless you. May He cherish and protect you a thousand times better than I could ever have done . . . George.'

I cannot bear it, she thought, I cannot bear it and go on living. She read the letter again, absorbing every sentence, every word, and though she could not accept all that he had said, she felt the rightness of the letter. Of course the affair had to stop. Playing with fire he had once called it. The time had come to put away the matches for good. She knew it and yet the knowledge could not deaden the pain. At least, she consoled herself, she had his child. She placed her hand across her still flat stomach. No one could take that away;

and George had recovered his health. That was important. He would go back to Joan and she would find him a softer, more compassionate companion. He had his God; she had his child. Neither of them had lost everything. It only seemed that way.

A beetle crawled across the floor of the summerhouse close to her feet. She saw it and she saw the dirt and cobwebs. There was a mound of feathers under a deck chair where Horrible had killed a bird. The tennis rackets and strawberry nets lay in a disordered heap. Somehow it all seemed indicative of her disordered affections. She pushed the letter into her pocket and her fingers felt the crumpled remains of the one she had received from her son that morning. She pulled it out and smoothed the single sheet. Fourteen days until they were all home. She tried to find comfort in the thought, but instead felt a mounting panic. It was not long enough for her to set both her house and her heart to rights.

On impulse she decided to clean the summerhouse. She worked furiously as if hard physical energy might help her to forget, but from time to time her tears fell, gathering the dust.

20

Next day she received a letter from Ken to say that he would not be coming home for another week and that he had made arrangements with a colleague to take the Sunday services. It was a brief letter which merely stated the relevant facts as concisely as possible, but she did not expect more. Ken did not usually write at all when in retreat. She put his letter down with a sense of relief. With Ken away she did not need to keep up appearances. She was glad of solitude in which to struggle with her unhappiness.

The next day or so were the hardest she had ever spent in her life. She lived on the verge of misery unaware of those with whom she came into contact. She gave lunch to the friendly young curate who came to do Sunday duty, but afterwards she would not have recognised him again. It was as if she were enclosed in a bubble of distorted glass through which no sound could penetrate, and through which people appeared shrunken and unfamiliar. She lived on the rarefied air of her own emotions.

She did not weep or hide from callers as she had done before her first visit to Lethey Bridge. She appeared normal, or so she believed. In fact, her life was turned upside down. Her daily routine of village and vicarage life had become the dream; the absence of George was the only reality.

A dozen times she started to write to him and as often

tore the sheet up and burned it. In an effort to put him out of her mind she threw herself into a frenzy of spring-cleaning. She turned out the attic rooms in a fever of impatience and drove Mrs Bews to sullen disapproval by enlisting her help to turn every carpet in the house. She washed walls, cleaned shelves, tidied drawers in addition to the usual chores. She could not bear to sit still or be silent. Her portable radio blared light music from all parts of the house during the day and the television flickered and chattered, until tired out by the exertions of the day she fell into an exhausted sleep. It was a crazy sort of despair and she did not know how best to cope with it.

She told herself it would pass. Deep down she knew it would pass; time would dull the memory and assuage the pain, but what to do during its slow passage was the question. Dimly and perversely, she realised that part of her did not want to stop suffering for when the anguish was over, the love would be over and for the time being she was not prepared to let go her love.

She wrote to Mary convalescing after her operation, but remembering her friend's agonised love for Jim, she was reminded of her own love and had to bring the letter to an abrupt close.

Clem was intrigued by her burst of energy. 'It must be the nesting instinct,' she said, 'but for Heaven's sake, don't go and overdo things. You'll be exhausted before the holidays start.'

Alison welcomed exhaustion for it left her too tired to think. Her bitterest grief was a fantasy woven round the night they had made love. If only she could have that time again, how she would have cherished and pleased him. Her waste of those precious hours seemed, in retrospect, unforgivable. George had told her not to dream. She knew her fantasies increased the anguish, yet without them, she could not have lived at all.

Time and again she rebelled against the code that held them apart. Why, she argued, should she not take happiness when it was offered as other women did? Why should the claims of her husband and children take precedence over the claims of her lover and unborn child? What made her so different from other wives who, after the unpleasantness of divorce, settled down to new and happier lives? George had said that she would never be content away from her family, but how did he know? Why should a first family be more important than a second? In the light of her conscience she knew all the answers, and try as she might, she could not stifle it entirely.

She had always believed that the particular agony of love belonged only to the young, that maturity brought with it a softening of sharp edges, a dulling of nerve ends, but she knew now that she had been wrong. Maturity brought with it a sense of responsibility which only increased the anguish. She had never felt like this in her youth, and she was glad. She might not have survived.

In the end, she took the car and drove into town. It was a blustery day with dazzling periods of sun between driving showers of rain. She drove fast, purposefully, and yet without allowing herself to recognise the reason for her journey until she arrived.

A car-park ran down the centre of the road where the vicarage stood. She found a vacant space some hundred yards beyond the vicarage and switched off the engine. It was a relief just to look at the house. She let her eyes rest on the windows, the door, the tidy square of garden in front of the house, the wrought-iron gates. She felt her body relax and her hands slackened on the steering wheel. She had no wish for the time being to do anything but sit and rest.

As she looked, the front door opened and Joan came out. She was, as usual, smartly dressed, and she carried an umbrella and shopping bag. She walked briskly in the opposite direction towards the shopping centre, her heels clicking confidently on the empty pavement. Alison's hands tensed on the wheel.

She knew he must be in for Joan had not attempted to lock the door when she left. All she had to do was cross the road, walk along the pavement till she reached the house, open the gate and ring the bell. She had done it so often in her dreams that it seemed only natural to get out of the car, lock it carefully and cross the street.

The sun had disappeared behind a surly cloud; rain plummeted down into her face and she ran the last few yards to the shelter of the porch and raised her hand to touch the bell. But she could not ring it. She stood there on the doorstep unable to make the simple movement required.

As she hesitated, she thought she saw out of the corner of her eye, the curtain at the study window move. She had a sudden mental image of the Dean standing there disapproving of her presence, willing her to go away. When she turned her head to look properly there was nothing to see; no one was there and there was no disturbance of the cream net hanging or the dark velvet curtain, nothing to indicate that anyone was there or that anyone had seen her.

Although she did not believe that the Dean had seen her and that the movement was anything more than a symbol of her anxiety or a strand of hair blown across her cheek, she turned away blushing with humiliation, and hurried back to the car. She switched on the engine and drove away without a backward glance.

She drove down the main street busy with afternoon shoppers, not sure what she was looking for until she saw it in the shape of his church. Here at least she had the right to enter. If he were to find her here . . . her heart leapt as a whole new range of possibilities entered her imagination.

The church was a Victorian mausoleum lined with brass and marble plaques erected to dead benefactors. Ornate and dark, it had nothing to commend it either architecturally or aesthetically. She sat down in one of the back pews and tried to picture him in front of the gilded pretentious altar. But there was nothing of him here, nothing of God either if it came to that. She walked up the aisle towards the choir-stalls, and opened the big prayer-book on his desk, but there was nothing, no name or inscription, to show that it was his. There was an assortment of hymn-books, lectionaries, psalters, Testaments on the ledge under his stall, some worn by years of use. She opened a shabby tuned hymn-book and saw his name on the fly-leaf. Her hands tightened on it and for a moment she was tempted to take it, but after a while she put it back, ashamed of such a childish impulse.

Apart from a palm cross, dry and yellow with age, which she found in a Bible, there was nothing personal, nothing to show that this was where he sat and worshipped Sunday by Sunday. She had no proof even that the cross was his.

The vestry door was locked, but she knew it would be as tidy and impersonal as his study had been. There was nothing in this sepulchral building to show he had ever been in it except for one hymn-book with his name on the front page. Even the notices in the porch were type-written. Shivering, for the building was as cold and dank as a tomb, she left not once glancing back.

Leaving the car conveniently parked outside the church, she walked towards the main street. There was always the chance they might meet. Would he stop, she asked herself, or would he lift his hat and pass on, and if he stopped what would they say to each other? Would they comment on the weather and lower their eyes to hide the unspoken thoughts? So engrossed was she in her fantasies that she did not notice Joan until they were face to face.

'Good afternoon, Mrs. Osmond. Blustery, isn't it?'

Joan smiled her tight social smile and was about to walk on, but Alison was too quick for her. Dear God, she thought, for this much I am grateful.

'Mrs Tindall!' she exclaimed, a little falsely. 'How nice to see you. Now I can take the opportunity of returning your hospitality. Come and have some tea with me.'

'How kind of you, but I don't really think . . .'

'Now please don't refuse me. It's not often that I'm in town. Besides, I want to hear all about the sale. It was a great success, I gather.'

The way to Joan's interest was direct and simple. It had not taken Alison long to find it.

'Oh well, if you insist,' she replied, not altogether ungraciously.

Alison led the way to a tea-room near-by. They found a table by the window and sat down, loosening their coats.

'Tea and cakes,' Alison told the waitress. For the first time in days her spirits lifted. She did not ask for news of the Dean directly. That was a treat to be held in reserve, like a birthday present to be savoured first in anticipation.

Joan bridled under her compliments about the management of the sale and launched into a long tale about the sins of one of the stall-holders. Alison did not listen. All the time she studied the carefully painted face for some indication of the state of her private life. Was she happier, or still anxious; tense or relaxed? Alison could tell nothing from her expression. She looked across at the well-groomed hands picking politely at a pastry, and envied them their various tasks. They washed his clothes, prepared his meals, made his bed. She envied this woman to the extent that she would have changed places with her, but she did not hate her. She wanted to be near her for she knew that this was as near as she would ever be to George. She thought up crazy schemes whereby they would become close friends meeting regularly, not for the purpose of conversation, but just to be near her. She would even be prepared to play bridge.

To her horror she saw that Joan was beginning to button her coat. She had not yet asked about George, and soon it would be too late. She felt in her bag for her purse, and while she was rooting for change to tip the waitress, she asked the question as casually as possible.

Joan replied in the same vein. 'Thank you, he's pretty well considering . . .'

'I hope you are managing to get him to take life more easily.' Her voice was shaking.

Joan laughed thinly. 'As well ask the moon to turn on its back.' She stood up and picked up her basket. 'I must rush. I've got an M.U. meeting tonight and George wants an early supper too.'

'Don't go – not yet,' Alison urged, with an edge of desperation in her voice.

Joan glanced at her curiously. 'What's the matter? Aren't you well?'

'It's nothing,' Alison said quickly, aware that she had been careless.

'You don't look at all well. It's your condition, I suppose.'

'I'm all right. Just a bit of a headache, that's all.'

'Are you sure? You could come back to the vicarage and rest . . .'

'No,' she interrupted sharply. 'No, thank you all the same,' she added more politely. 'I promise you I'll be all right.'

'Well, if you are sure . . .'

'I'm fine. Please don't let me keep you. You must be very busy.'

Watching her go, Alison wondered why she had turned Joan's offer down so quickly. She imagined meeting him in Joan's presence and could see the anxious question in his eyes. As she unlocked her car five minutes later, she came to the conclusion that unless they could meet honestly, she did not want to see him again. She had had two opportunities that afternoon and had turned them both down. And yet she still yearned for him. If there was no relief to be found in seeking him out, where then was she to find relief?

21

Although Alison knew that her inability to allow herself to see the Dean was a form of pride, such self-knowledge did not lessen her unhappiness. Rather it increased it. Before her visit to Coolwater Bay, she had been able to live in anticipation of the possibility at least of seeing him again. She had held the prospect of what could happen as a last resort against despair, but now that she had been and found the visit fruitless, her unhappiness was the greater for being without further hope of alleviation. She felt feverish with frustration.

If only she could have gone to him and told him honestly of her state of mind he might have helped her, but this she was not prepared to do. Such a confession of weakness might lessen his image of her and she preferred to keep her unhappiness rather than risk losing his respect.

That evening Clem phoned. 'Can you do my Red Cross drive tomorrow, darling?' she asked anxiously. 'Honey's developed a sore ear and I must take him to the vet. I'll do your turn next week.'

Prepared to do anything to distract her thoughts, she agreed to go. She and Clem and several other women in the village took it in turn to drive handicapped children to the nearest special school for bi-weekly therapy. It involved picking the children up from their homes in nearby farms and villages and taking them into town. It was a task Alison usually enjoyed for the children so obviously looked forward to the small outing.

It was a clear fresh morning with a touch of late March frost when she set out. The world was gleaming and fresh as it must have been on the first day of creation. In the midst of the fresh spring morning she felt that she alone was old and dreary. The cool greenness and crisp light seemed to mock her depression and the contrast between herself and the glorious world was unbearable. She tried to lift her thoughts out of the depths of despair by thinking of her sons. It was only a week till their return and she tried to devise treats in her mind for the short hectic weeks of vacation, but, like homing pigeons, her thoughts kept returning to George. She had reached a high peak of desperation.

A cat streaked across the road. She swerved automatically to avoid the creature and found herself in a queasy heart-stopping skid. The road for about a quarter of a mile was a rink of treacherous black ice.

'I'm going to die,' she said out loud, but with surprise rather than terror as the car continued on its uncontrollable journey. There was nothing she could do. The vehicle had taken on a lunatic life of its own. Suddenly it seemed to leap into the air. Gorse, grass and hawthorn rushed towards her. The sky expanded and exploded in a burst of light. There was a distant noise of breaking glass and she knew no more.

When she swam up out of the dark sea of unconsciousness, strong arms were lifting her out of the wreckage. She found herself looking into the face of a local farmer whom she vaguely knew. Usually it was cheerful and ruddy, but now it was pale and creased with anxiety. Someone tucked blankets round her and the family doctor was holding her pulse. His quiet voice repeated reassuringly that she was fine and that as far as he could tell there were no bones broken. She heard and saw without comprehension. She felt cold and could not breathe properly. As she was lifted into the ambulance she slipped back into unconsciousness and when next she opened her eyes she was in hospital. Two warm-fingered nurses were undressing her. She heard one of them say:

'I'll have to fetch a pad. Her period's started.'

'But that's impossible . . .' Alison started to say, and tried to lift her head until a sharp intense pain blotted out conscious thought.

After a while she was aware of a cool hand on her head.

'Are you awake, dear? It's all right. There's nothing to be afraid of. You have had an accident and concussed yourself slightly. We want you to lie quite still and try not to worry about anything. You are going to be all right.'

She could feel the pad between her legs and the contracting pain in her womb no worse than a usual menstrual nag. Tears seeped through her closed lids.

'Let the tears come, dear,' the nurse said with compassion in her North-country voice. 'You've had a nasty fright. Just let the tears come.'

She kept her eyes closed while the doctor prodded and pushed with gentle knowledgeable hands.

'We've sent for your husband, Mrs Osmond. He'll be here this evening.'

'You shouldn't have done that . . .' she began, but did not continue. Suddenly she wanted Ken with an uncomplicated wholly dependent longing.

'I want you to have an X-ray, Mrs Osmond. I don't think there are any bones broken but we want to make quite sure.'

Her bed was wheeled into the X-ray room by a young Irishman who whistled and teased the nurses. It seemed incredible to her that anyone could feel so cheerful. She was lifted on to the X-ray table and a young white-coated radiographer arranged her body for photographs.

Presently the young woman put her head close and said brightly, 'Not a bone broken, Mrs Osmond. You've been very lucky.'

It was not worth arguing.

When next she opened her eyes Ken was looking down at her.

'I've killed the baby,' she told him.

He touched her clenched hand and she turned her head away in an agony of grief.

'I wanted him so, I wanted him, I wanted him.'

'I know,' he said gently. She turned to look at him and saw that there were tears in his own eyes.

His tears seemed strange to her. She had never really thought of Ken in relationship to the child and she had not thought of him grieving at its loss.

The sister returned with a syringe. 'I want to give her a sedative, Mr Osmond. Perhaps you could return later? She ought to be kept as quiet as possible.'

He bent and kissed her briefly. When she opened her eyes he had gone.

'This will make you feel better,' the sister said. When Alison did not reply, she added, 'You've had a bad shock. It's only natural that you should be upset.'

When she awoke it was night. A nurse was bending over her and smiling. She recognised compassion in the smile and had the urge to weep but no tears would come. Her eyes were sore, her throat dry and her cheeks stiff with salt.

'Are you feeling better?'

She moved her head fractionally.

'You'd like a drink, I expect.'

'Don't go.' Alison touched the cool smooth fingers. She wanted to talk to this gentle anonymous human being. 'I've lost my baby,' she said.

'I'm so sorry – but look at it this way. It might have been your life.'

'I wish it had been my life.'

'You don't really mean that.'

'How do you know?' Alison asked because she was curious to know how this girl would reply.

'Life is always precious even when there's only a spark left in a tired sick old body.'

Alison turned her head away. The explanation was too glib, taken from a text-book. What could this girl know of such matters?

'I'd like some tea, please.'

'Of course. I'll get it.'

The nurse returned with the tea and sat down while she drank it. 'Have you any other children?' she whispered.

Alison nodded between sips of the hot sweet liquid.

'How many?'

She did not seem surprised when Alison told her. She did not even hint that five was enough surely for anyone. Suddenly Alison found herself talking about her sons.

'You don't look old enough to have a grown-up son. My boy-friend's twenty, but his Mum looks like a real Granny beside you.'

Aware of the girl's transparent effort to cheer her up, Alison could not help smiling.

'Is he all mod – you know, with long hair and the gear and everything?'

'I suppose he is.'

'And don't you mind?'

'Not particularly.'

How ridiculous, Alison thought. This child should be having the heartaches, not me. I'm just somebody's boyfriend's mother to her. She smiled again and the nurse was charmed, believing in her own therapy. She bounced with confidence as she took the cup back to the kitchen. Alison fell asleep again, but the tears flowed all through her dreams.

Clem called in for a moment the following day. She was laden with spring flowers, glossies and guilt.

'Darling – I feel so wretched! If I hadn't asked you to do my turn . . .'

'Then the accident might have happened to you and what would that have solved?' Alison replied, but even as she said it she knew, had known all the time, that the accident would not have happened to Clem. Ever since George's letter had come, she had been heading for some sort of disaster. She cringed inwardly, imagining Dr Pearce's contempt. She was not capable of committing suicide honestly. She had to wrap it up in an accident, in which she had killed the child instead of herself. She did not deserve to be alive. In that moment she realised that the night-nurse had been right. She was lucky to be alive, glad even to be alive. For the first time she began to feel better.

Visiting hour came and the ward filled with mothers and aunts and friends bearing laden shopping baskets and bedside smiles. She watched the door, confidently expecting Ken, but he did not come. It was the Dean who came.

As she watched him cross the ward, she wondered if this perhaps had been the true motive behind her accident. It had brought George to her. Yet now that he was here looking down at her she felt no quickening of the pulse, or flush of excitement. She felt nothing.

'I've lost the baby,' she said before he had time to greet her.

'I know.'

He brought a chair over to the bed and sat close to her. She stretched out her hand to him on the white counterpane and he covered it with his own. His fingers were warm and strong and his touch completely impersonal.

'I'm sorry,' she told him. 'I wanted your child – but you know that.'

'Perhaps it's for the best.'

She had thought that she had so much to say to him, but now that he was here, she could think of nothing. Her hand felt uneasy in his.

'This past week,' she began, 'it's been unbelievable. I did not know there could be so much unhappiness. I tried everything to help me to forget.'

'Did you try God?'

She looked up at him quickly and realised with a shock that he had come to visit her as a priest, not a lover. She had a crazy urge to laugh.

'What has God to do with it?' she asked, drawing her hand away.

'I'll tell you if I may.'

He pulled his chair closer and began to speak words of encouragement and exhortation. All the time she was thinking how much he had changed. This was not the man who had turned to her in love and despair. This was certainly not the man with whom she had fallen in love. This stranger was a priest fulfilling one of his priestly duties, 'Visitation of the Sick' as it was called in the jargon. He had no need of her, and as she listened to his voice pronouncing the pious sentiments, she realised an even greater truth. She had no further need of him. She had had a certain need of the child and as long as he had existed, she had wanted his father. She knew then from personal experience what George himself had once told her, that nothing remained static, least of all the delicate fluctuating emotion of love.

'George,' she asked curiously, interrupting him, 'would you give me another child?'

He smiled faintly. 'You haven't been listening to a word I was saying, have you?'

He was right to ignore her question. She had no more wish to conceive again than he to beget.

'It's been a strange affair,' she said, looking at him as if for the first time, yet knowing that she was speaking to him for the last time.

'God has turned it to good account,' he said.

'Do you really believe that?' she asked, trying to keep the incredulity out of her voice.

'I know it,' he replied simply, 'and so will you, in time.'

'Perhaps,' she said to please him. She did not think she would ever believe it.

She thought he would go then, but instead he shifted nervously and his expression changed.

'Alison,' he began uneasily. 'I have something to tell you. I believe, I hope that you are strong enough to hear it.'

'Tell me,' she said, unalarmed, knowing that nothing he could say to her would have the power to make her suffer again.

'I've been offered another living.' He paused, waiting for her comment, but when she did not reply, continued, 'My uncle's parish has become vacant. Some of the older members have remembered me from when I stayed there as a curate and asked if I would be interested in the job.'

'And are you interested?' she asked.

'Yes . . . yes, I am.'

'Where is it?' she asked.

'Scotland,' he said quickly. 'It's a beautiful place in the

Highlands with mountains and a fishing loch on the door-step.'

'Scotland,' she repeated quietly. She would never see him again.

'Yes,' he said seriously. 'It seemed to me to be the answer.'

'Will Joan like it?' She could not see Joan on Scottish hills.

'I believe so. She's Scots by birth, you know. Her people came from Edinburgh.'

She looked at him and smiled. 'If you're happy, then I'm happy for you, George.'

'Then I can go with an easy heart.'

The visitors' bell rang and he stood up ready to go.

'Why did you come?' she asked curiously, as she remembered her own reluctance to seek him out.

'Kenneth rang to tell me about your accident,' he said, replacing the chair.

'Ken?' She felt cold.

'He asked if I would call.'

'Why should he do that?'

'Is it so strange? After all, one of my duties is hospital chaplain.' He seemed surprised that she should be upset.

'Did he tell you about the baby?'

'He said that you had miscarried, yes.'

She closed her eyes. Dear God, she thought, he knows.

'I must go, Alison.'

'Yes, of course,' she said quickly, wishing he would leave. She was suddenly impatient for him to get out of her life before he wrecked it altogether.

He put his hand on her head and gave her a priestly blessing. She was aware of her creased brow under his hand. Oh Ken, she thought, remembering how he had looked at her bedside the previous day. She realised that his happiness mattered more to her than her miscarriage, more than the news of George's departure. At last she was beginning to see her life in its true perspective and she knew that Ken and her marriage were what really counted. She could not bear the thought of his knowing about her disloyalty and his hurt at what she had done.

She tossed and turned in the hospital bed until the evening visiting hour. He was not among the other husbands who trooped self-consciously down the ward with flowers and fruit clutched awkwardly in cellophane wrappings. Her eyes never left the swing doors of the ward. Her head ached with concentration, but he did not come. After a while she knew that he was not going to come and she wove one fantasy after another in which he accused her, left her, took her sons from her.

The night-sister gave her a sedative and she fell into a deep exhausted sleep.

22

The following day she was discharged from hospital. Ken came for her in a borrowed car. Anxiously she searched his face, but she could not tell by his expression what he was thinking.

He told her that there were letters from the boys giving them the times of their trains. They would all be coming home in four days' time, after which the eldest was going to Paris for Easter with a friend, and the second on a geological course for five days. The third wanted to bring a friend back for the latter half of the holidays and the fourth had been in the San for a night with a bad throat. Ken's voice went on and on in unaccustomed verbosity and she had the impression that he knew she wanted to talk seriously, and rather than risk hearing what had been too long hidden, he preferred to keep the conversation on a trivial level. Perhaps he was right; perhaps it would be wiser to say nothing, to stay on the undemanding non-communicative level they had settled for years before.

So she let him drive her home without saying what she believed was uppermost in both their minds. Mrs Bews had prepared a meal for them which they ate quickly and without enjoyment. She could see that Ken's uneasiness was increasing and her own had just about reached breaking point. Just as a love affair could not remain static, nor could marriage. She and Ken had to move on to a new relationship even if the effort of doing so threatened to destroy the relationship they already had. She put down her coffee cup with a small clatter and was about to speak when the telephone rang.

It was to ring intermittently all afternoon with anxious inquirers and friends curious to know all about the accident. Mrs Smiley called as did several others who stayed and gossiped until the early evening. Ken disappeared into his study as usual. When at last she was alone again she was tempted to let the whole matter drop and she would have done so if she had not felt so lonely, and that in spite of the fact that she had been surrounded by warmth and kindliness all afternoon. She stood outside the study door for several minutes before she could bring herself to go in. In her imagination it reached the proportions of a stone wall matching the mental barrier that seemed to exist between them. It took all her strength and courage to open it.

He was sitting in front of the electric fire staring at the glowing bar. As far as she could tell he had been there like that all afternoon, for the pile of letters that had accumulated over the past week were still lying unopened on his desk.

'Ken,' she began, 'I've been meaning to ask you – what made you tell the Dean to visit me yesterday?'

She was filled with bravado, determined now that she had begun to go through with the whole thing.

'So he came,' he said evasively.

'Why did you tell him about the child?'

'George is a good fellow. I thought he might be of some help to you.'

He was still being evasive.

'Was that the only reason?' she asked, and added when he hesitated, 'Ken, I've got to know.'

'What other reason could there be?'

He sounded genuinely surprised, and she believed that

he was telling the truth, and yet she could not think it was as simple as that.

'What could the Dean do that you could not do?' He was silent. 'I really want to know, Ken,' she insisted.

'So,' he replied quietly, 'you want to know; at last after all these years you really want to know something that concerns me.' His tone was not bitter, but she sensed his sadness.

'I don't understand,' she said hesitatingly.

'I don't suppose you do.'

'Won't you explain, then?'

'Explanations can sometimes do more harm than good.'

She sensed that he was talking about something even more serious than her affair with George. 'Not in this case,' she argued.

'Perhaps you're right. Perhaps we have not aired our linen enough over the years, but I don't want you to be hurt.'

'Hurt!' she exclaimed. 'I don't believe you could ever hurt me, Ken.'

'Then my task is easier, for if I've lost the power to hurt you, then I have already lost your love; where there is no pain there can be no real love.'

'That's not what I meant,' she cried, but he paid no attention.

'There has been no love between us for a long time,' he continued. 'I'm right, am I not?'

So now it was coming. She felt nauseated.

'I'm not blaming you,' he said. 'You had too much to do with the children. I should have been more help to you, I see that now. You didn't have enough love for me and the boys so I was the one – necessarily – to be ditched. I didn't need you as they did.'

She was astonished. 'I never stopped loving you, never!' she insisted.

'Not consciously perhaps. All the same I came to matter less and less to you. I was someone to wield the heavy stick on the rare occasions when the boys were too much for you. I was the one you all paraded in front of – with unconcealed reluctance – every Sunday morning in church.'

She began to see that what he was saying might well be true, and she was shocked once again at the depths of her self-deception. Just as she had been amazed when Dr Pearce had pointed out that she had fallen in love with the Dean, so she was equally amazed to recognise the fact that her marriage was dead, and had been so for as long as she could remember.

'Why didn't you say something? Why didn't you tell me?' she cried.

'Yes,' he said with a sigh, 'that is the question I've been dreading, the one I would prefer not to answer.'

'But you must answer it!'

'When you stopped needing me – as a stud . . .'

'Ken!' she exclaimed, shocked.

'I repeat, when you stopped needing me – I stopped needing you. As the years passed I realised I should never have married. I was not the sort to make a good human partnership. In the early days I sometimes used to be bitter about being pushed out of my own family. Those outings and picnics which were arranged without consultation with me, because it was always taken for granted that I would be too busy or too tired to come. I used to feel that I was not wanted by any of you until I grew to realise that no one pushed me. I edged out by myself. I promised myself that as soon as the boys became independent, I too would become independent. Ever since Christmas I have been trying to find the right opportunity to tell you that I wanted to leave you.'

'To leave me?' She could not grasp what he was saying. 'A divorce, do you mean?'

'I was thinking more on the lines of a private separation.'

'But where would you go?'

'Into a monastery. I believe that I have a vocation – that I always did have a vocation which I refused to listen to when I was younger.'

'But what about us? The boys and me?'

'You have enough money of your own to manage and the boys are all at school. You no longer need me, if indeed you ever needed me.'

'I had no idea,' she said, amazed and shocked. 'I had simply no idea you felt like this.'

'Surely you must have realised that we were not particularly close?'

'I suppose I did,' she agreed reluctantly, 'but I thought that was the way you wanted it.'

He stood up and began to move about the room. 'I wanted to escape. How I longed to escape! The noise, the bickering, the smell of food, the banging doors, the eternal tooing and froing of noisy children that seemed to be no part of me and my life. I could not wait to escape.'

'What stopped you?' she asked, close to tears.

'You started another child. I know you didn't tell me about it at first, but I knew probably as soon as you did. I had been expecting it for years, ever since the birth of the last boy. You suck the life out of me to make your sons. You are all woman, all womb, all mother. There was even a time when I believed that you started this child on purpose to prevent my escape. I blamed you for causing another obstruction to what I longed to do. I was sick with hate and blame.'

She remembered how he had leaned over the kitchen sink after she had told him about the child, grey with nausea.

'Yet you still slept with me. All those years wanting to leave me and yet you still made love to me. I don't understand that.'

'I'm a man,' he said simply, 'and you were there.'

'No more than that!' she exclaimed. 'Sex without love all these years while I . . .' she broke off remembering that as yet he knew nothing of her abortive attempt to find sexual pleasure without the trappings of love.

'Habit, I suppose.'

'I never so much as guessed . . .'

'Surely you must have sensed that something was wrong when I went into retreat?'

'But you go into retreat every year.'

'Not in the middle of Lent,' he said gently.

'You weren't going to come back!' she exclaimed, as the truth became apparent. 'I'm right, aren't I, Ken? You were going to stay indefinitely at that retreat house.'

'That would have been impossible,' he said with a faint smile. 'I went there to try and sort myself out. Truthfully, I don't know now what I would have done.'

'And then I had the accident and you had to come back in a hurry.'

She saw it all now, the reason why he had not visited her in hospital. Those stagnant tears that had been there for the whole of their marriage. She was filled with compassion for him, and sorrow for herself.

'You don't have to stay,' she said, turning her head to hide the rush of tears to her own eyes. 'There's nothing to keep you now. As you said, the boys are at school and I can manage. Will you resign the living?'

She picked up a scrap of paper from the floor and began to tear it into small pieces. She knew the time had come to tell him about George, but she could not trust herself to speak.

'No,' he said gently. 'I was able to think things through when I was away; that and your accident have helped to put matters into a certain perspective. I see now that I've been mainly responsible for the chasm between us. You did not withdraw from me. I withdrew from you. You did not monopolise the children and leave me out – at least intentionally. I left you out of my life first. If I had been kinder, if I had been here, you might not have had the accident and lost the child. I owe you my life for his life.'

Now was her chance and she took it.

'No, Ken, you owe me nothing.'

If he wanted an excuse to leave her she would give it to him. It was the least she could do.

'The baby had nothing to do with you.'

Now it was his turn to look bewildered. 'What on earth are you talking about?'

'It's true. The child was not yours.'

He sat down, at a complete loss for words.

'So you see,' she continued. 'You are quite free to go to your monastery.'

'I drove you to that?' he said incredulously.

She smiled faintly. 'I can't even offer that as an excuse. It happened because at the time I wanted it to happen.'

'Who was it?'

'Does that matter? It's over now.' She had the Dean's permission to tell him the truth, but she was reluctant to involve him now that the affair was dead.

'It was Jim, wasn't it? You stayed there when you were in

Pendale. He's always been interested in you. He once told me that if he'd met you first . . .'

'It wasn't Jim,' she said firmly. The distaste, dislike even, in Ken's expression made her all the more determined not to bring the Dean into it, if possible. It was better that Ken's jealousy – if that was what it was – should be directed towards a faceless nameless stranger than towards a colleague whom he respected and liked.

'Don't force me to tell you, Ken. Believe me, it can't help in any way.'

He saw that she meant it and cried harshly, 'I can't believe it. I can't believe you capable of such an act – you of all people!'

'Do you really mind so much?'

'I mind very much indeed. Did you think I would not? Did you honestly think I would condone your sickening adultery? Did you think at all?'

'Why should you mind?' she retorted, her anger rising to match his. 'I'm not jealous of your God and He is a great deal more dangerous to me, it seems, than George could ever be to you.'

In her anger she had said his name and Ken was quick to notice.

'George?' he said, incredulity taking over from anger. 'George Tindall? I can't believe it.'

'It's over, Ken,' she said, her anger equally deflated. 'Believe me, it's over for us both.'

'He was a sick man – out of his right mind – or was it perhaps this that . . .' he broke off, shocked to the soul.

'We were both a little out of our minds at the time,' she said sadly. 'I'd rather not talk about it.'

'Oh, Alison,' he said, looking at her with wretched eyes, 'we are in a mess.'

'I know.'

It was the first important decision they had made together in years. Suddenly she felt very tired.

'You're free now. You can go to your monastery as soon as you like. You owe me nothing.'

He shook his head. 'How can either of us be free stuck in this slough of muck? If you've been unfaithful to me, I've been equally unfaithful to you. If you drove me out of love with you, I certainly drove you into love with George. We helped each other into this mess and we've got to help each other out. Until then there can be no talk of freedom. We are chained together until we are able to leave each other with love . . .'

'I don't want you in chains,' she cried.

'Do you want me at all?'

She looked at him and saw not only the amalgam of her five sons, but a glimpse of the individual she had married.

'I have always wanted you, I think. There are no chains where I am concerned – but what of you?'

'It is possible to learn to love one's chains.'

'So what do we do?' she asked.

He reached out and took her hand, holding it between both of his own. 'We try again, a little harder this time.'

23

She saw George once again. The station was full of parents as she waited for the school train to arrive. Her three younger sons were among the first to get off the train. Her heart beat faster as she saw them, gangling, untidy, with shy wide grins, as they clambered on to the platform clutching an assortment of grips, parcels, cases and a coffee table made at carpentry classes, and inadequately covered with a piece of dirty sacking.

'Damn and blast,' said her youngest, already beginning to show off. 'I've lost my ticket.'

'Can I drive, Mother?'

'Don't be an ass, you haven't got your provisional licence yet.'

'I'm starving. Can we go and get something to eat – now? We've had nothing since seven this morning.'

'Try your back pocket.'

'It's got a hole in it.'

Other parents smiled at each other over the heads of their sons. Every year they shrank a little as their sons stretched.

It was then that she saw him. He was coming out of the Enquiry Office, and he saw her in the same moment that she saw him. He stopped and they stared at each other over the heads of the milling passengers. He raised his arm slightly in a gesture of greeting and at exactly the same moment, she raised hers. All the time they looked at each other, she was aware that she felt nothing, neither regret nor relief, only a vague sort of disbelief.

'Wake up, Mum, you're dreaming.'

She turned to look at her youngest son.

'I've found my ticket. Guess where?'

When she looked back again, he had gone. As she opened the boot of the car for the boys to stow their luggage and listened to their loud young talk, she was not sure whether she had really seen him at all. He had become as insubstantial as a ghost. The memory of all that had happened between them was meaningless, to be resurrected perhaps in the dark hours of night when fantasy took over from reality. In those dark intimate moments there might even be flickers of regret, but not now. She breathed deeply as she prepared to plunge into the present. The long Lent term was over.